Scott blanched. "I didn't know she was married!"

"Yes, you fool." Wayne was shouting, when he suddenly remembered the guards. "And don't you realize what's happened? She overheard something, something that frightened her so badly she's about to do something desperate!"

Wayne motioned to the buildings behind him and to the men standing, talking in hushed tones. "There are too many of them. They're all over the place."

Scott looked totally stunned and miserable.

"You know," Wayne finished, his voice shaking, "you know what's going to happen, don't you? She's going to get herself killed trying to save us all!"

AMANDA CARPENTER, who wrote her first Harlequin romance when she was nineteen, was raised in South Bend, Indiana, but now lives in England. Amanda endeavors to enhance the quality of her romance novels with original story lines and an individual style. When she's not writing, she pursues her interests in art, music and fashion.

Books by Amanda Carpenter

HARLEQUIN PRESENTS

703—THE WALL
735—THE GREAT ESCAPE
759—RAGING PASSION
919—WAKING UP
991—ROSE-COLOURED LOVE

HARLEQUIN ROMANCE

2605—A DEEPER DIMENSION
2648—A DAMAGED TRUST

Don't miss any of our special offers. Write to us at the following address for information on our newest releases.

Harlequin Reader Service
901 Fuhrmann Blvd., P.O. Box 1397, Buffalo, NY 14240
Canadian address: P.O. Box 603,
Fort Erie, Ont. L2A 5X3

AMANDA CARPENTER

reckless

Harlequin Books

TORONTO • NEW YORK • LONDON
AMSTERDAM • PARIS • SYDNEY • HAMBURG
STOCKHOLM • ATHENS • TOKYO • MILAN

Harlequin Presents first edition February 1988
ISBN 0-373-11047-2

Original hardcover edition published in 1986
by Mills & Boon Limited

CHAPTER ONE

LESLIE looked around the crowded disco inter-estedly. People always fascinated her, no matter what they were doing, whether they were working or playing, loving or hating. It was why she had gone into journalism, the people. And the dance floor was certainly packed with them. The music was so loud that the beat pounded in her chest, the song powerful and elemental. Her foot tapped on the floor, and she looked around to grab Wayne's hand.

'Come on!' she said to him. 'I want to dance.' He obligingly followed her out on to the floor, and Leslie let go of his hand. She started to move, her body graceful, eye-catching, swift and sure. She danced well, having a natural aptitude for rhythm that had been enhanced by lessons, and she threw her soul into it, abandoning herself and laughing with brilliant eyes at the man who grinned to see her enjoyment.

She worked very hard and now it was time to play hard, for she had some rare time off, and she intended to take advantage of it while she could. She was going to enjoy herself and stay out all night if she wanted, and do whatever her mood prompted her to do. She was free for three days, for a lifetime, and she wasn't going to stop until she dropped. After the dance they went back to their seats and ordered drinks, Leslie feeling flushed and thirsty.

'You'd think we see enough of each other on assignments!' she said, laughing at Wayne. 'But here we are again, Laurel and Hardy, Batman and Robin——'

'—Tweedledee and Tweedledum,' he finished drily. 'I know it. But we're a nice pair, we work well and compatibly together, and we like to play together occasionally, too, that's all.' It was true. Wayne and she were good buddies and a good work team. They'd worked side by side for nearly three years now, and they knew each other's method of thinking, and reasoning. Being newspaper reporters for a nationally syndicated paper was no easy task when you happened to be a foreign correspondence team. It called for leaving at the drop of a hat, and going wherever one was sent. It called for a cool, clear head under pressure and for quick thinking in times of potential danger. It called for trusting one's work partner. He had to be there when you needed him. And you had to be there, in just the same way, stable, constant, and loyal.

Wayne was a good photographer and they worked on a basis of mutual respect. Leslie had the cool, clear head needed for her particular brand of journalism. She had an unshakeable steadiness running as a stable underthread in just about everything she did. She held on to her perspective, she reserved judgment, and she was able to quickly grasp essential facts. She was also a bitingly sarcastic writer when aroused, if someone or something met with her criticism.

'May we join you?' A smooth voice interposed through their light chatter, and they both looked up simultaneously. Leslie's face immediately closed up, wary. The two men who stood in front of their table also worked for the newspaper as a journalist team, and they were good, very good. The taller of the two men, Jarred Caledonia, was the speaker. She didn't know either one very well.

Wayne stood up politely. 'Please do.' And he turned to signal for a cocktail waitress. Leslie nodded to the two men and tried to remember the shorter man's name. She couldn't, which made her angry at herself, for she prided herself on her ability to remember names and faces. She smiled at both of them and said nothing. 'So, Jarred, Scott,' Wayne said easily, sitting back down. 'How's everything going? You two are just back from Turkey, isn't it?'

'That's right,' the shorter man spoke, and his voice was lower than either Wayne's or Jarred's. Scott, Wayne had said. Leslie mused. That's it, Scott Bennett. He was very good. She liked his work. The man was incredible, had a mind like a ferret when it came to information. His ability to find underground sources and new facts was legendary. Her respect for him, now that she knew his identity, increased several notches. 'And from the looks of things, we're going to be heading back in a few days.'

'What's happened?' Wayne asked interestedly, and Leslie's mind began to wander impatiently as the three men started to talk shop. She'd just had a harrowing two months, catapulting all over South America, El Salvador in particular, and she'd been in a constant state of tension and wariness in that troubled, volcanically explosive country. She didn't want to talk work. She wanted to have fun and forget the vastness of the upheavals in the world. She wanted to dance and drink a few drinks, and maybe drink more that a few drinks, and to laugh and have a good, funny conversation. Maybe she could go to a matinee film tomorrow afternoon, and then see another tomorrow night. She was behind in her film going since she'd been out of the country, and there were some good flicks playing in the theatres. She should try to catch them before she left.

She stood, a quick, fluid movement, and restless. 'I don't know about any of you,' she said teasingly, interrupting the men. 'But I'm going to find myself a partner and dance the night away. You can talk shop all you want. Not me, sirs. See you!' And with an airy wave, she started to head away from the table.

Her arm was taken and she turned to see who had touched her. It was the taller man, Jarred, and he smiled down at her easily as he said, 'I can't blame you for not wanting to talk about work when such energetic music is playing! If you would be so kind . . .'

And as the music was right and his manner so

appealing, she laughed and bowed mockingly at him; in answer he bowed back. They went out on the dance floor and she turned to face him, steps light, movements compelling, her smile a vivid white. And she put a lot into that dance. She knew that he noticed and appreciated it, as did several other men nearby, for while she danced and moved lightly around him on the floor, never stopping or pausing, and while her actions seemed carefree and even frivolous, her mind never stopped working, storing data for further perusal. That was essentially Leslie. She never stopped watching and observing, even while she cajoled and charmed.

One thing Leslie didn't notice, though, was that she and Jarred were being watched by the two men back at their table. She didn't see their eyes on her slim, quick figure, bright in a provocative summer outfit. She was certainly worth watching, for though in repose she could never be called beautiful, she was eye-riveting, and Leslie was never out of action. Movement was her life, and it showed in every gesture and laugh, every sparkle from her dark blue eyes. Scott's eyes still followed her, the whip-like fluidity of her dancing, her chocolate brown hair bouncing with vitality around her vivaciousness in a perfect dark frame, when Wayne turned to say something to him.

Leslie noticed her fresh drink at her empty seat when she and Jarred returned to the table. 'Mm, thanks, Wayne,' she murmured, picking up the glass and drinking thankfully. It was gin and tonic, her usual.

'Can't take the credit, babe,' she was told cheerfully. Her eyebrows rose in surprise, and she looked at Scott for a moment, silently questioning. He inclined his head, smiling crookedly.

'You're welcome,' was his deep, easy reply to her repeated thanks. Her eyes, which had lit on him in an impersonal and friendly way, became arrested on the man's face. At first glance, Jarred was perhaps the more attractive of the two, but the other man certainly bore up well under scrutiny. Though shorter than Jarred, he was definitely the more powerfully built, with long, sensitive fingers on large, capable looking hands and wide, heavily muscled shoulders over lean, trim hips. His hair was nearly white from being bleached in the sun and in contrast his skin was nearly mahogany in colour, and his eyes were a dark, velvet brown, unusual with the skin and blond hair. Just now those eyes were holding an unmistakable, but subtle message as he smiled into her eyes. At least she thought that he'd smiled, but his facial expression had never shifted. Very subtle, she thought, and after the first arrested moment, her own dark blue eyes became amused. She held his glance a moment as she smiled slowly at him, and then she drank delicately from her glass.

It was convenient, she thought, that he should be sitting right by her. It took barely an effort for him to start a low voiced conversation with her, with that heavy, loud music in the background. They were quite effectively in their own little world, with the noise and the crowd of chattering, vivacious people. He leaned both arms on the table, bringing his head very close to hers, and he asked her quietly as he caressed her with his eyes, 'You're back from a hard stint of work yourself, aren't you?'

They talked a while, getting to know each other somewhat better. She was in a conversational mood and murmured the right things at the right time, meanwhile smiling at him with her eyes, fully aware of what he was doing.

He asked her, 'What was your last assignment like?'

'I talked to villagers whose homes had been destroyed in El Salvador. We've an article and some photos on one of the families. The mother is a widow and her two sons have been shot. Her daughter is eleven years old and suffering from malnutrition. The village is rubble.' Leslie spoke emotionlessly. Her bitterness and rage had gone into the succinctly biting article she had written. It had been taut with the suppressed fury and energy she had held in all those weeks, afraid to display it, intent on keeping a low profile. It was, she knew, very good. And her emotions were back in rein after what she'd seen. Her eyes bounced sharply off the thoughtful man beside her, taking in with a lightning swiftness his irregular features, the tough, once-broken nose, the lean muscled jaw, the forceful forehead. Time to change the subject. 'I like your work,' she told him candidly, letting her simple admiration show through for a moment to add sincerity to her words. 'You've been in the business for some time now, haven't you?'

'Around eight years, I'd say,' he replied offhandedly, taking a quick drink from the beer he held cradled in his two large hands. She noted the clean, well kept fingernails and approved silently. You can tell a lot from a man's hands. 'Before that I was a business executive.' His eyes went to hers mockingly.

She didn't let him see the surprise that she was sure he'd expected. She had heard something of the like at work. 'Makes for a diversified life,' she returned laconically, tilting her head and examining the archway adorned by two plants. They were fake. Scott must be around thirty-six or eight then, she mused silently. Without looking at him again, she stared at the tiled floor beneath the archway and thought that he was in very good shape for someone beginning to see the approach of the forty year mark. Very good shape indeed.

Her thoughts halted right there, and she took a deep breath as she felt the tightness in her chest, her mind. Control it, she told herself. The music pounded through her veins and the room was hot. The room was very hot and too crowded, and she didn't like all those people anymore. She smiled at Scott warmly just for the sheer hell of it, just to throw him off, and then she said quite pleasantly, 'Good night.'

She turned and said goodbye to the other two men who'd been talking animatedly at the other side of the table. Wayne nodded, knowing her too

well to say anything or be surprised at her abrupt
departure, and Jarred said a polite farewell also,
not knowing her well enough to be surprised.

She stood, nodded at Scott silently, noting his
lazily raised eyebrow, and knowing that the wheels
were clicking away in his head over her strange
departure. She turned and walked lightly to the
exit, swinging the shoulder length hair off her neck
and feeling the slight dampness at the nape, under
the heavy mass. Outside she paused at the front
door, seeing the black of night and the glare of
bright lights. Chicago was hot this summer, she
thought, lifting the hair off the back of her neck
and thinking without pleasure of her uncomfortable, empty apartment. No air conditioning in ninety degree weather, cooped up in that
small living space, torture. Heat.

As she paused on the pavement, undecided, she
heard a footfall behind her. Across the parking
lot, a car tooted its horn. Traffic was heavy on a
Friday night, in this part of the city.

Scott's deep, lazy voice said behind her, 'And
what are you planning to do now?'

Leslie stood still for a split second and then she
stretched deliberately while she held the heavy
weight of the hair off her neck, fully aware that
Scott was watching her body and slightly appalled
at her own recklessness tonight. She smiled.
'Probably go home and take a long, cold shower,'
she sighed. 'Then get out, dry off, and do it again.'

She didn't look at him. Traffic sounds in the
background. Dead silence between them. 'My

apartment has air conditioning,' he said softly. It was an invitation and she turned to stare at him, eyes giving nothing away. 'You could come over for a nightcap if you'd like, and cool off for a while.'

A moment, at once quickly gone and yet so slow in going. Leslie looked around, warring within herself. You know what he's asking, she whispered to herself silently. You learned your lesson once, girl. You'd only needed to learn once in the past.

She stared out into the black and glaring night, feeling the heat, the humid, sticky evening. An almost instantaneous succession of images flashed in her mind, the last being her empty apartment. She took a deep breath, feeling the muscles in her chest move, her lungs work, and then she turned slowly to look at Scott, at his wide, powerful shoulders and those trim hips. He was taller than she by a half a head, and much heavier. His legs were long and lean, as were hers. She smiled with her head half tilted at him, feeling his eyes on her, watching her, quietly waiting. 'I'd like that,' she said.

His apartment was spacious. She looked around in appreciation at the furnishings. It was a quiet place, much like the man himself. He moved to the kitchen and came back with an iced glass of gin and tonic, and something for him. She guessed it was whisky, as she took her drink with a thanks. It was a nice blend. He had a light touch, then. She smiled at him slowly, felt his eyes on her lips, and then turned away to walk aimlessly through the living room.

'Your apartment's very nice,' she told him lightly, touching a heavy antique with a slim, stroking finger. 'The executive position must have paid well.'

'It paid enough,' he laconically agreed. He was behind her and she hadn't heard any movement, so presumably he was still standing where she'd left him, probably sipping from his glass. She didn't turn around, mildly diverted by her guessing game. A rustle of carpet and he was moving over to her left. A chink of glass on table. He was coming her way. She didn't move, waiting for him to stop behind her. He did.

'When do you leave again?' she asked him.

'I don't know. Probably in the next few days,' he replied automatically. She felt her stomach quiver with a laughter she wasn't sure was unassumed. The laughter was probably a product of the tension, she thought. Even so, she didn't even jump when his hand came down gently on her nearly naked shoulder, stroking the still heated skin lightly, fingers cool. 'Where have you been in the last eight years?' he asked softly, voice deep, slightly amused. 'How could I have missed you all that time?'

The last eight years. She laughed quietly, and knew that Scott took her laughter in an entirely different way than as she'd meant it. That soft laughter hadn't been amused. That soft laughter hadn't been nice at all, if he'd only known.

Leslie had been in the mood to swing either way. She really might have backed out before that moment. She truly hadn't expected to give into this crazy, wild, utterly foolish impulse. But everything had led up to this moment, this man, this way of life. And something gripped her, something new. She leaned ever so slightly into the palm of his hand as he stroked her back delicately, and she turned her head to look into his dark, lovely eyes fringed with darker blond hair. She could see herself in tiny twin reflections as he watched her. She'd decided to be alone for the rest of her life. She could still be alone, but she didn't necessarily have to be lonely. He was a male, and he was very attractive.

Their eyes held, and then he was moving his head down very slowly. She knew what he was doing. He was giving her a way out, giving her time to react and decide. She smiled again, put up her hand and fitting it to the back of his head, feeling the cords of strength in his muscle, and the silky warm, silver blond hair flowing over her fingers. She applied gentle pressure, and smiled as he complied to her persuasion. His mouth covered hers, moved, and then he was deepening the kiss and pulling her body into a tight, close fit against his. She tasted whisky in his mouth.

She was unsurprised by the passion that gripped her in a slow mounting wave. She'd found this man attractive from the first, and she was well aware of her own sexual desires. What frightened her was the intensity of her need, and her feelings were consuming her self-control. She'd wanted to be in control, and now she knew she wasn't.

She tilted her head and couldn't hold back the moan that rose from the back of her throat as Scott slanted his mouth down her neck, hitting the sensitive cords. No matter, she thought hazily, as he bent and picked her up with a suddenness that caught at her breathing. There would be time enough for control in the morning. She held on to his shoulders as he strode on down the hall and into a dark, shadowed room. He deposited her on the bed and remained bent over her for some time just looking at her, trying to make out her expression. Then his hands went to her shirt buttons. She sat up and helped him.

Leslie was awakened in the middle of the night, in the very blackest of hours, by a large, calloused hand gently cupping her shoulder and pulling her around to face the man she was sharing the bed with. For an instant she froze in heart-stopping disbelief as old memories flooded back from a past that was no more. It couldn't be! Then awareness hit her and her body relaxed again as she drew in a deep, shaky sigh. It wasn't. Time had not rolled back. The past was truly past, and she was in bed with a man who had given her much pleasure. His hand roamed over her and, feeling his desire and her own again, she rose up on one elbow to kiss him, hair spilling over his face and shoulder. His hand came up and held her head in place as he deepened the kiss. Then he was pushing her back against the pillows and coming up from his reclining position to tower over her. She could see the moonlight hitting his right shoulder, making the warm skin seem like marble. She reached up and put her lips there. The skin was silken. There were no words spoken.

Leslie very slowly moved off the bed while her eyes never left the sleeping face of the man with whom she'd just spent the night. Scott lay with the sheet twisted around his hips, his naked shoulders wide and dark against the utter whiteness of the sheet underneath him. His arm was flung out. It had just covered her a moment before. His silver blond hair was tousled, and his rough face relaxed. She hadn't disturbed his slumber.

She gathered up her clothes and crept into the bathroom, where she hurriedly washed and dressed, combing her hair with rough, impatient strokes. She was sore. Then she went into the kitchen and made a pot of coffee, having a quick cup herself and leaving the rest on the warmer. It would be ready for him when he awoke. After that, she went to the living room, slipped on her dress sandals, picked up her handbag and silently left the apartment.

She had to take a cab back to the parking lot where she'd left her car. She made the drive back to her apartment in record time, anxious to be back in the solitude of the living space that she'd dreaded last night. She parked her car, ran up the stairs, and unlocked her door. When she was finally inside and locking the door behind her, the enormity of what she'd done hit her and she sagged against the wood, aghast. Incredible, she thought, how could I have done it? A trembling spasm rocked her.

But she knew. She knew and understood herself, which made it no easier to take. It had been four years since Dennis and Jennifer had died, four full, action packed years. After the shock and the grief had subsided, they had become good years. She'd become successful in her job. She loved her work.

But the four years had been lived alone. She'd had no one to share her bed with. She'd made good on her own and loved her freedom, but she had been married once, and had known her own sexuality, had felt it awakened. She'd known what it was to make love with a man, and last night her longings had simply overcome her. She wasn't proud of that. She should be in better control. Others may slip up, but not her.

Oh, Dennis. Jenny, Jenny ... Her eyes filled with tears and she moved away from the door like an old woman. She went through the small apartment and into her bedroom, over to her dresser. She picked up a framed photograph with hands that shook, while the ache in her heart felt like a heavy, hurting stone. There they were, the two of them. Dennis was laughing, tall and lean and darkly handsome. Jenny stood hanging on her father's legs, begging to be picked up. She was three in that picture, just barely three years old, with beautiful blonde wavy hair and a beautiful, sunny smile. My Jenny, Leslie thought, and the tears came again.

They were both so utterly dead.

She would have been seven. She would have been going to school and coming home each day, laughing her wonderful laugh, spreading sunshine better than the sun. She would have been right there for Leslie to hug and love, if it hadn't been for the accident.

That icy winter day and the pond down the hill from their house. She had come home from a day at college, the term nearly over with. Christmas vacation nearly on them, and no shopping done yet. That snowy white day had been the blackest day of her life. Down at the pond there had already been a crowd of people, for several boys had gone to play and found the ice broken by two bodies. She would never see her Jenny again, never feel that warm, wriggly body hurtle against her for an exuberant hug, never see her running or playing or laughing or loving again.

And Dennis. Leslie still felt guilt about Dennis. She sat on the bed and carefully wiped a tear off the photograph. Dennis had been so handsome and kind, and so very patient with Jenny. In the beginning Leslie had thought their marriage was the most wonderful thing that had ever happened to her. She'd been just twenty-one to Dennis's thirty. She had adored him, and he had genuinely loved her. That first year was one of her happiest memories, filled with joy and love and the excitement of her pregnancy.

It was hard to pin-point when things had changed. She still wasn't sure when it had happened, still couldn't decide. She had gradually grown into a self-confident, capable woman while Dennis had still seen her as a rather shy young girl. She'd wanted to explore the world, wanted to see things on her own and with Dennis, wanted to share her growth with him. But gradually she had come to realise that he was stubbornly holding on to his image of her when they'd first married. And she was no longer that girl.

Her family had loved him, absolutely worshipped the ground he'd walked on. After the first tentative expressions of restlessness, Leslie had kept her feelings to herself. Her sisters hadn't wanted to hear. Dennis was the best catch in the neighbourhood, the area, hell, the whole state. He had a fantastic, well-paying job. Leslie didn't even have to clean house if she didn't want to. He adored her, everyone could see that.

He'd just adored her for the wrong reasons. Leslie had finally managed to go to college after a great deal of cajoling and pouting, pleading and wheedling. She was bored. She only wanted a class here and there, to keep her occupied, like tennis classes or dancing lessons. Finally he had agreed, and she had gone to college, picking up classes a little at a time, surreptitiously and systematically getting the credits that she needed for an English major and her degree and lying through her teeth about it to everyone else.

Emotional blackmail is a funny thing. Now

Leslie felt a slow burning rage at herself and everyone else who had conspired to keep her in her place, to keep her in the niche they had carved for her. But at the time she'd been genuinely trapped. She'd felt trapped because she'd truly loved Dennis, loved him for his gentleness and his kindness, loved him for his good-natured disposition and his faithfulness to her. She'd felt trapped because she could really understand his bewilderment at the changes in her. She'd felt trapped because she couldn't see leaving him and depriving Jenny of her father's daily, steady influence.

The last few years before the accident had been such a mixture of pleasure and pain, the good and the bad, the contentment and the stifling cage. Leslie looked back and could see that she'd been heading for a crisis, that she and Dennis would have had a head on collision sooner or later, that things couldn't have continued the way they had.

And she felt so horribly guilty because she felt such a release at his death. It was a terrible thing to even think, she mused, feeling the guilt lurk at the back of her mind. She'd never in a million years have wanted him dead. She had loved him. She had loved Jenny so very much, and even now missed her so badly it ached. But she knew that she missed Jenny far more than she did Dennis, and that made her feel like dirt.

Leslie sat on the bed and remembered how she had wandered around the empty house for months in a state of numb shock after their deaths. She remembered the tears that wouldn't fall for a long time. She remembered how she had then cried hysterically when she finally walked into Jenny's room to clear away the toys and the clothes.

She hadn't felt free even then. She had looked ahead at the blank future and felt a crippling fear. But somehow she had got through that first year, had got through the last few courses in college and graduated, four years older than most of the others in her class. She had put their lovely old house up for sale, gritted her teeth and went recklessly up to Chicago to look for a job.

Everyone had said she was crazy. They'd said that she'd be back within a few months, and why for God's sake would she want to work when Dennis had provided for her so generously? She had listened politely to what everyone had to say, packed her bags, and had gone anyway. She was good. She'd been a good student and was good at writing, and knew it. Everyone at home had been surprised when she had landed the job at the *Chicago Times*, but she had never had any doubts about it. If it hadn't been the *Times*, then it would have been someone else, for her mind was made up. She wouldn't have stopped trying until she secured a job.

The last three years had been wonderful. She was eager for every adventure, every new experience. She had to go out in the world and see as much as she possibly could. It was in her blood, so deeply rooted that she would never get it out. She was really free for the first time in her life. She threw herself into the job with such energy and enthusiasm, and she was one of the best reporters that the *Times* employed. She was respected and liked, and she was good.

She was twenty-nine and alone. She was reaching the best years of her life and she wasn't going to wreck it now by getting trapped again, by being stifled, pushed down, smothered. She wouldn't think of last night and her loss of control. She wasn't going to look back; ahead was where everything was for her.

Her finger went out and caressed the cold, impersonal glass in the frame. Jenny.

CHAPTER TWO

LESLIE walked down the hall with the swift and easy movement of a woman in shape and in control. It was, for a change, cool and cloudy outside, and so she had on a black sweater and slacks, with a plain, severe white blouse underneath. The outfit was saved from utter severity by a single pink rose in full bloom tucked into the lapel of her open necked shirt. Her dark brown hair was up in a business-like knot, and her eyes were alert, expectant.

She always felt this way after a nice rest from work. She was always eager to get back to the grindstone, to wrestle with issues, to grapple with her limited understanding of the hugeness of the world. She walked without hesitation into an empty conference room and threw down her handbag. Then she moved over to the window and started to fight with the stubborn window catch that always stuck before giving reluctantly. It finally opened with a protesting screech, and she pushed the window wide with a sigh as cool air wafted into the room almost immediately. She inhaled with appreciation and then turned around calmly. She didn't know why afterwards, when she thought of it. There had been no sound.

Scott leaned against the closed door, his rough

features impassive, eyes thoughtful as they travelled down the length of her and then back up to her face. One wide, strong shoulder was higher than the other, and his arms were crossed casually. He didn't move.

After the first startled instant, her own face smoothed into inscrutability, eyes slightly amused as she regarded him gravely. She wasn't acting the amusement. She was indeed feeling a certain bitter irony at herself and this man, and the whole intensely uncomfortable situation. She'd always been so sure she would not be caught in something like this.

The silence had at first been contemplative, and now it became acutely heavy, and her eyes had lost their amusement as she tried in vain to think of what he was wanting, looking for. That he was looking for something, she had no doubt, as his eyes searched her face over and over again.

She grimly decided to break that heavy silence, which had become terrible. 'Hello,' she said, with deliberate inanity. Kill him with superficiality, she thought, and it put the gleam back into her blue, blue eyes. 'How are you today? And how on earth did you know where to find me this morning?'

'I talked to Carl,' he replied simply, saying a lot with that line. So he knew her editor, did he? He was still watching her, and it was getting on her nerves.

'I'm getting briefed for a new assignment,' she continued conversationally, moving away from the window and perching on the edge of the table. She

started to swing an idle leg back and forth,
watching her slim foot. 'It will be interesting to see
just where I'll end up going this time. Did Carl
already tell you that?' she asked him innocently,
and looked up to see his lips tighten slightly. She
smiled at him slowly, using her own brand of
surface charm, and she could see that he was
getting angry.

'Thank you for the coffee you made before you
so abruptly left,' he said politely. The very tone of
his statement made it both an accusation and a
question.

'You're welcome,' was her bland reply. 'I helped
myself to a cup, so it wasn't a totally unselfish
action. Do you think it will rain?'

'I have no earthly idea.' She could almost hear
his mind work behind the impassive exterior. She
couldn't blame him. If she'd been in his shoes, she
would be trying to figure her out, too. Her
amusement deepened at the thought. When he
reached the conclusion he was meant to reach,
he'd be hopping in the other direction like a cat
who'd touched water, and trying to get away from
it as quickly as possible. 'Would you have dinner
with me tonight?'

'No, thank you,' she told him with a studied
politeness. 'I'm busy.'

No change in expression, just those dark,
watchful eyes. She suddenly had a furious desire to
see his face change, but controlled herself as best
she could. What was he thinking? 'Would
tomorrow suit you better? I know a place where

we can sit back, relax, and just talk.' His quiet, unemotional voice had a peculiar inflexibility to it, and her eyebrow rose as she realised that he was going to push it.

'I am,' she said very gently, 'going to be very busy every night from now on.' Though her tone was gentle, her eyes were not, and they watched him every bit as alertly as he watched her. She was, for some strange reason, beginning to feel distinctly wary. 'Thank you very much, anyway.'

'Perhaps lunch would suit you better, then,' he continued, and she felt a wave of anger at his deliberate obtuseness. He knew what she'd meant. The man was intelligent. She didn't deign to reply but merely shook her wrist out and looked at her slim gold watch with impatience. Wayne and Carl were to have been here ten minutes ago. 'I took the liberty of informing them you would be a half an hour late,' Scott said calmly.

Her temper nearly erupted. Calm down, Les, she told herself. This is one time when anger will get you absolutely nowhere. Her eyes were attracted to his figure as he shifted in a lazy fashion and stood upright, the slight movement rippling muscles under the thin cotton shirt. Her attention became diverted by a sudden, unwelcome memory of how silky his skin was and how thin the veneer over hard, unyielding muscle. Warmth flooded her and her cheeks tinted lightly pink. She cursed inwardly at herself and him, for his eyes had never moved from her

face and she was positive he had seen her blush.
'I don't eat lunch,' she returned, shutting her
teeth with a decided snap.

'Pity. You're too thin.' He cocked his head to
one side and studied her very seriously, while
Leslie fought to control her conflicting urges.
She wanted to hit him for his provocative
behaviour, and she wanted to run as fast as she
could away from him. That brought her head
up. He was the one who was supposed to be
doing the running. Her eyes narrowed. 'It's
funny, but I just hadn't figured you for the sort
of person who goes in for one night stands,' he
continued in that easy, pleasant tone of voice,
and she suddenly realised that he was utterly,
totally furious with her for walking out without
saying goodbye or at least saying something to
him, the day before yesterday.

'If I'd thought it was going to be anything but
a one night stand,' she retorted tartly, shooting
him a sharp glance, 'I wouldn't have done it in
the first place.' His facial bone structure seemed
to go rigid, and her brows rose. 'Oh, does that
bother you?' she murmured, mockingly com-
miserate. 'I hadn't realised you were that sort of
person.'

His eyes shuttered, and the very lack of
expression in them threw a chill over her like
nothing she'd ever experienced. He was not only
furious, he was actively battling with his rage right
in front of her, and she'd mocked him too far.
'Sometimes one can be surprised out of first

impressions,' he said unemotionally. 'I just hadn't
figured you for a——'

'Whore?' she supplied helpfully, furious now
herself. He just looked at her. She realised his
hands were curled into fists. 'Don't, please, make
value judgements, will you? As I recall, you issued
the invitation.'

'But now I'm wondering who seduced whom?'
He arched an eyebrow at her, and she wished that
she was a thousand miles away from this scene. It
could be arranged, she knew, and the amusement
was there again in her eyes as she realised that
she'd soon be far away. Soon everything would be
put into perspective, and she could put her awful
mistake behind her. His question she didn't even
bother to answer, as they'd both been active
participants. She winced at the thought. Contrary
to what he was bound to believe, she had never
slept with anyone beside her husband.

'Well,' she said briskly, pushing off the table
and standing upright herself. 'I can't say it's been
pleasant, because it hasn't, but at least we know
where we stand now.'

'Do we?' he asked strangely, cocking his head
to one side. 'Somehow I don't think we both do
and, at the moment, I have no idea which one of
us it is. You are a strange mixture of contrasts,
Leslie.' She felt an unexpected quiver run
through her at his easy use of her first name and
the bizarre combination of intimacy and aliena-
tion she felt for this man. It was awful. 'And
the only thing I can think is that I'm not seeing

the whole picture of you just yet. I wonder what I don't know.'

'Nothing important,' she murmured, feeling deep alarm. Nothing important. Her sweet baby. A lance of old pain shot through her and it showed very briefly. His eyes sharpened. 'I really must cut this short,' she continued determinedly, gritting her teeth. 'I do have a job to do.'

And with an impersonal nod, she picked up her handbag and started for the door. She had to walk by him and suddenly she couldn't, as he whipped her around with a swiftness that took away her breath, and his head darted down as he pushed open her lips and kissed her deeply, furiously. Her head fell back, and she nearly lost her balance. His hands snaked around to her back and gripped her firmly. After that first stunned moment she tried to jerk away but couldn't, and so she kissed him back just as furiously. She nearly fell again as he took his hands away and stared at her.

After the first stunned moment, he just softly laughed and shook his head. 'I've work to do, too,' he told her, while she shook with rage and reaction. He crossed to the door and opened it, looking back briefly. Something showed in his eyes and then was gone. 'I'll be seeing you, Leslie,' he said, and she knew that he fully meant it. He left the room.

'Damn him to hell,' she told the room conversationally, but only she was there to hear, and she really knew that she was damning herself and taking all the blame.

After a few minutes, she felt recovered enough to go look for Wayne and Carl. She found them talking, or rather arguing, across the desk in Carl's office. They both turned when she entered. 'There you are,' said Carl irritably. 'It's about time you got here.'

'What do you mean?' she asked. 'I've been to the conference room and you didn't show up.'

'Scott Bennett told us you'd be late and so we've been talking over things in here while we waited for you.' Carl surveyed her speculatively, and she flushed with annoyance. Wayne's eyes slid away and she glared his way for a moment.

'Well, Scott was wrong,' she replied tartly, moving over to a chair and angrily sitting. 'I've been waiting in the other room, so why don't we get on with whatever we're supposed to be doing?'

Carl tossed her several pages of typewritten paper. 'Before we get on to the new assignment, I want you to rewrite this,' he told her in a no-nonsense voice. Wayne threw up his hands in disgust and turned away, while Leslie frowningly looked through the pages of her last article.

'Whatever for?' she indignantly asked. 'I worked my——' She caught sight of Carl's stern, waiting face. '——my tail off on this.'

'It's too emotional,' he told her flatly and sat back for the explosion.

'Like hell it is!' She bounded up in anger just as he'd known she would, and for the next ten minutes argued hotly about the merits of her article with Wayne indignantly interposing his own statements from time to time.

'We won't use it until you rewrite it!' Carl finally said firmly, and Leslie snapped back at him:

'It's damned good and you know it!'

'Of course it is, you idiot! But it's still too emotional!'

'It's angry!'

'I know it! So sit down and cut it out!'

She suddenly quietened and got really serious, feeling much better for letting off some steam. 'Is it really that heavy?' she muttered, looking through the pages. 'I thought I'd handled it well.'

'It's beautifully eloquent, and it's too much, Les. You've got to be more dry, simply stating the facts. Toward the end let yourself be a little bitter if you like, but only about human conditions, not about politics. This isn't an editorial, it's a news article.' Carl sat back and drummed fingers on the desk as he waited.

She sighed, resigned, knowing he was right. 'All right. I'll get it done by the end of the day.' She peeped at him from behind the papers she was perusing.

'I need it by two this afternoon,' he said, and actually winced as he waited for another explosion.

This, however, she'd been expecting. 'Slave driver,' she muttered bitterly, but stood and headed for the door. She grinned as she left the room. Wayne and Carl were already arguing about something again.

'On my desk at two o'clock, finished!' Carl

roared after her. 'And be here at two-thirty for the briefing of your next assignment, do you hear?'

'Don't push it, Carl!'

She was done and on time, and she had a half an hour to herself. She nipped down to the canteen, picking up a sandwich and a cup of coffee and heading for an empty table. After a quick glance at her watch, she wolfed the food down and decided to take her coffee back up with her. She hurried for the stairs.

That afternoon she found out that she and Wayne were supposed to be going to South America the next day via New York, and she nodded, unsurprised. One was sent where one was familiar with the language and people, and she did speak fluent Spanish. She had hoped for a change, though. 'At least it's not El Salvador,' she muttered.

'Argentina.' Carl was crisp. 'We want you to get the general flavour of the country and its mood. Dig into it, and the Falkland crisis. Get the commoner's opinion about it, and play up the human interest. Get reactions to the rebellions— use your head and sniff around. You'll be down there for a month or two, and of course if you get wind of something that might take you out of the country, use your judgment and go for it, if you think it's best. You have my cautious blessing. Also . . .' As Carl talked and rounded the corner of his desk, Wayne looked over to Leslie and crossed his eyes. She stuck out her tongue at him. 'Wayne!' Carl barked, seeing the one but not the other. 'Could you control your puerile tendencies, if you don't think it would strain your I.Q. too much?' Leslie grinned.

After their briefing, Leslie asked him curiously, 'Why, oh Great One, are we being shipped via the New York persuasion? Why not to Miami or one of the southern airports? Would it be more direct?'

'Yes, it would be more direct!' Carl mimicked her tone of voice and she laughed at him. 'It was the only flight that I could get you on tomorrow. You two have had enough time to waste as it is. It's time you were back to work! You're changing planes in New York. Here are your tickets ...' And the rest of the afternoon passed in an energetic haze of activity as Leslie rushed around to get everything ready for her departure the next morning. She was leaving again. It tingled all through her every time she thought about it. Everything would be fine.

But that night, as the night before that, she tossed and turned and couldn't get to sleep as she thought of the one man she would dearly love to get out of her mind. She wondered if he was sleeping with anyone else that night, and if so, with whom. She couldn't wait until tomorrow. Then maybe she could get him, and herself, and what they'd done out of her mind.

She was packed and ready, so all she had to do in the morning was shower and get dressed, leaving her hair wet and hanging down her back. It would dry soon enough and she wasn't taking her hair drier with her, anyway, so she would have

to get used to it again. There was no telling where
they were going to end up, and the drier was extra
weight. She couldn't know how prophetic her
thoughts were at the time. And when she did
realise it, the irony of the situation and the danger
drove any possibility of amusement right out of
her mind.

But this morning she had no inkling, and all she
knew was that she was going to have a long hard
day of travelling ahead of her. She dressed
accordingly. Gone was the sophisticated woman
from the day before. Today she had on a pair of
khaki slacks and a sleeveless cotton shirt, with a
khaki jacket slung over her arm as she headed out
her door, only one piece of lightweight canvas
luggage with her and a carry on filled with a tape
recorder, plenty of batteries, and all of the
stationery she would need. Travelling light was
something that she had become used to some time
ago. It was surprising how many pairs of slacks
her lightweight luggage piece would hold. Her only
luxuries were some blusher, eye shadow and
mascara, and her photo of Dennis and Jenny.

She was meeting Wayne at O'Hare and started
to look for him the moment she entered the
terminal. He was not yet there, she saw, as she
made her way through the throngs of people. She
had plenty of time, so she checked her luggage in
and then headed for the magazine stand, pur-
chasing several to keep her occupied while she
waited for the flight and for Wayne.

Once she thought that she felt appraising eyes

on her, but when she looked up, she found no one she knew close by, and so she soon dismissed it from her mind. It was getting close to boarding time, and he still wasn't there. She stood, reluctant to miss the flight and loath to board without Wayne. She flicked her wristwatch up, an impatient movement. There was time to make a call, to see if he'd left his apartment or not.

Just as she'd turned towards the row of telephones, she heard a shout behind her and turned back around. Her heart gave a great lurch and her world swayed a moment before righting unexpectedly, and she fervently hoped that her discomposure hadn't shown on her face, for there walking towards her was not only Wayne, but Jarred and Scott, and they all had luggage in their hands. Just as the suspicion hit her mind, she dismissed it, telling herself that it couldn't be, but there Wayne was, explaining that they'd got caught in traffic, but at least they hadn't missed the plane, and Leslie began to realise that Scott and Jarred were on the same flight to New York that they were. She took a deep breath. It was only for a few hours, she thought consolingly, while her eyes bounced to Scott and then off him again. Then she and Wayne would be getting off and taking another flight south while Scott and Jarred continued to London and from there to Turkey. They might not even be sitting together.

Scott hadn't even looked at her, as he surveyed the crowds of people, the babble of voices both foreign and domestic, his head thrown back, feet wide apart and well planted. He had on a pair of faded jeans, very tight, with a white cotton shirt that emphasised his dark tan and rugged, uneven features, and his silvered hair that was carelessly brushed back. It curled under, low on his neck, giving him a leonine appearance. She quivered, and wondered that no one else could see the powerful tug of attraction she felt for him.

Somehow, she wasn't sure how, she managed to say in a calm, neutral tone, 'I'll just have a seat then, and wait for you to check your luggage on.' Wayne nodded to her, Jarred grinned, and they all took off for some time.

She looked up as someone paused by her and she smiled politely at Jarred, wondering inwardly how much Scott would have told him about their encounter. The euphemism she used made her smile grimly. News teams were by nature usually people who got fairly close. She wondered if Scott knew how to hold on to his tongue, and it struck her that she knew very little about him. She shook her head impatiently. She didn't want to know him. It had all been a mistake. How many times had she to convince herself of that?

Her restless gaze wandered over the people in the noisy, uncomfortably hot airport and she saw Scott and Wayne talking some distance away, both men with their back to her. She let her gaze wander freely over them both, and then realised that she was staring mostly at Scott. She made her gaze return to her magazine. Then the two men were sauntering over and it was time to board the plane. She stuffed her magazines into her bag, readied herself with her ticket. Scott was just behind her, with Wayne and Jarred following, and she quickly went down the aisle to her seat, waiting resignedly when she saw the three men following her. She wasn't surprised. The seats had all probably been booked at the same time, so naturally they fell together when possible. She was rather discomfited, though, when she found herself seated by the window and Scott's lean form easing down beside her. Her eyes flew to his impassive face. Was there possibly a hint of satisfaction there? She told herself she was imagining things. Hold on to your cool, Les, she whispered silently. You're losing it.

His legs took up a great deal of space and brushed against her, the thigh hard. She busied herself with arranging things in her bag and taking her magazines to stick them in the pocket of the seat in front of her. Then, checking to make sure she had her press pass, batteries and stationery, she closed the bag. Scott had already deposited his hand luggage underneath his feet, tucked into the provided space, and he sat back with his head resting against the back of the seat, legs stretched as far as he could get them, eyes closed. On the other side, Jarred and Wayne were talking with low voices. Trying very hard to relax herself, she sat back and watched the people at they were boarding.

She found plenty to keep herself entertained. Up ahead was the boarding entrance, and a harried looking flight attendant was talking in a low voice to a red-faced, indignant lady accompanied by a smallish, rather embarrassed man who had a peculiar habit of blinking rapidly behind his eyeglasses, giving him the appearance of being perpetually close to tears. Just behind her two young girls were arguing vehemently in rather loud voices as to which one would get the window seat. To the right were three children and their mother, the oldest child around twelve and the youngest still in nappies. She looked tired already, and Leslie's heart went out to her. Her attention was snagged by a flight attendant walking down the aisle, coming their way. At first Leslie's eyes lit upon the young lady disinterestedly, but then her gaze sharpened in speculation. The attendant not only looked hassled, as many attendants do especially after a long and hard flight, but this one looked positively haggard. Her complexion was pale and her eyes showed strain, and her mouth was held so tightly that there was a thin white line around the edges. She put up a hand as she passed Leslie's row to tuck up a stray strand of hair, and her fingers as they touched her temple were trembling. Leslie's brows drew together into a slight frown. The girl was obvious under a great deal of strain.

'And what's caused you to look so forbidding?' Scott's voice queried softly just by her ear. She jerked in surprise, and forced herself to relax, her face to calm.

'Nothing of importance,' she replied composedly. 'You switched seats with Wayne, didn't you?'

'What do you think? How long are you going to be in Argentina?' A quick turn of the head to stare at him, and Leslie found it a big mistake, as she was staring into warm, velvety chocolate eyes only inches away. Her eyes skittered away only to light upon his mouth, firm and yet mobile, and now slightly crooked at the edges. She knew that mouth. Utterly shocked at her own reaction to this man, she jerked her gaze away and had to ask him to repeat his question.

'God only knows,' was her short reply. She then sat back and buckled her seatbelt and did her best to project a repelling attitude. She might have known that he wouldn't even deign to notice her efforts.

Then the hatch was closing and the flight attendants were walking briskly about, as engines started to a high pitched whine. The plane lurched, and then moved gently away from the boarding apparatus. She gripped the sides of her seat tightly as the attendants went through safety procedures that she never bothered to listen to anymore. How many times had she flown? A dozen? No, more than that. Two, three dozen times? She had no idea, but it didn't matter, for the take offs and the landings always petrified her. Her fear was consistent, she acknowledged grimly, slowly paling. She had to give it that. It hit her every time. Usually Wayne was there to talk her out of it, keep her mind occupied, but now he was sitting on the other end of the row. She stared straight ahead as the plane began to hum even more, and the captain came over the intercom to wish the passengers a good flight. She leaned her head back against the seat and closed her eyes, willing the sickness to go away.

'Are you all right?' The question came from Scott, and was sharp. She nodded tightly without looking. The plane was now taxiing to the runway and was about to start taking off. Her hand was taken and held firmly, Scott's large hand a warm shock to her cold, tense one. 'Good Lord, your hand is like ice! Leslie, are you okay?'

The low concern in his voice caught at her attention and she reluctantly opened her eyes. Instead of looking to him, she found her eyes drawn to the swiftly moving scenery outside, and she took a deep, shaking breath. Then Scott's voice came, calm and reassuring, and he told her to look at him, not outside. She slowly complied, and then she did nothing but stare into his steadying, comforting gaze while he talked softly to her of God only knew what. She didn't know, for she just listened to the sound of his voice while the plane's power built up into incredible speed, pinning her against her seat, holding her down, and she fleetingly wondered what all of that power would be taking her to. The thought invariably hit her at this time, for she was now powerless to turn the plane back, totally at the mercy of the huge machine.

As soon as they were in the air and more or less

flying levelly, she wriggled her fingers in pro-
testation of his hard grip and sighed limply.
'Thanks,' she muttered, 'I'm all right now. It's not
bad at all when we're up, but the going up and the
coming down really get me.' Colour was coming
back into her face and she could breathe normally
again, instead of feeling as if her chest had a tight
band of steel around it. She grinned ruefully.
'Wayne is usually there to hold my hand.' She
looked past Scott and found Wayne looking in
concern around Jarred. She wrinkled her nose at
him and he laughed.

'You're full of contradictions, aren't you?' Scott
said quietly, and the statement brought her eyes to
his face, surprising a contemplative, searching
look. 'There's a lot I don't understand about you,
Leslie Tremaine. Quite a bit, I'd say. Just about
everything about you, except for your work.
You're crystal clear in your work.'

Her face closed warily, and she drew back from
him as far as she could get. 'I'm no enigma, no
contradiction,' she denied flatly. 'And I don't need
for my actions to be dissected into tiny bits. I am
what I am, and nothing you do or say is going to
change it. I'll be going to hell my own way, like
everyone else in this world, and it's nobody's
business which road I take.'

'Nobody's business?' he mocked gently, and his
gentleness was more unsettling than anything she
could produce. Then mockery went away, and he
was left to stare at her seriously, somehow sternly
as he said, 'And of all the different aspects of you

that I'm just getting to know, that is certainly the most pitiable.'

Leslie kept her head turned to the window and she stared out at the fluffy, thick looking clouds. They looked so real, it seemed that someone could jump from the plane and bounce in their mass instead of dropping right through and sinking like a stone in water. It was, she knew, going to be a long flight.

CHAPTER THREE

By the time the plane was nearing New York, Leslie felt like she'd flown half way around the world. She was limp and strung out from being continuously tense beside Scott. He, quite infuriatingly, seemed very much at ease, with legs sprawled carelessly out and his head tilted back. He treated her with a careful courtesy that was in itself an insult, and occasionally she saw fleeting flashes of that inexplicable anger he felt towards her. What was wrong with him? she wondered irritably. What was he expecting after such a night? What possibly could have developed from a night like that? It had been all wrong from the beginning. The only reason she could come up with for his behaviour now was that he was piqued because she'd left so abruptly. Strange situation, strange, uncomfortable man. On the one hand he treated her with thoughtfulness and on the other he treated her with sarcasm.

The seatbelt sign came on again, and people returned to their seats. Leslie tightened her belt again, feeling that familiar tension at the back of her neck. It had been a lousy flight, she thought glumly. That was for sure. She looked up and around the cabin and saw three men standing close to the strained-looking attendant, talking in undertones. She didn't look any better than before. Another attendant came up to the men and one of them gestured his intention to go to the front of the plane. She shook her head, and then he came very close to her, his larger body blocking Leslie's view of the smaller woman. They both turned and headed to the front.

Her interest piqued, she sat up straighter, eyes alert. The two had disappeared behind the screen at the front. Then Scott said something in a sharp low tone to Jarred, and she turned to look at him enquiringly. He was sitting up, eyes hard, body taut, one hand going to run through his hair carelessly. 'Something's ... going on,' he was saying. Leslie only caught snatches of it. '... don't like this one damn bit.' His hand went to his seat buckle as he stared at the slight female attendant beside the tall, dark haired man who then turned to survey the cabin of people with hooded eyes. His gaze seemed to halt a moment on Scott, and then move on. He turned and headed quickly up to the front of the plane. Scott said something under his breath that was muffled, and then both he and Jarred were jerking off their seatbelts only to stop stock still when a voice came over the intercom. It was not, Leslie noted, now totally bewildered and sharply alarmed, the voice of the captain. Her eyes slewed back to Jarred and Scott, who were rigid in their seats.

'Ladies and gentleman, we are now about to land in New York for a brief refuelling.' The voice was crisp, slightly accented, business-like, male.

'At that time, most of the passengers will be asked to disembark, except for thirty and the flight crew, who will be the hostages of the People's Revolutionary Republic. Do not get out of your seats. Do not come to the front of the plane or you will be shot. Do not harm or distract the flight attendants as they come around.' Without further ado, the intercom was switched off, and everyone in the cabin was left to look around them in bewilderment, horror and dismay.

Scott swore viciously under his breath. Jarred said to him in an undertone 'There was nothing we could do. We weren't expecting it to be this way. There are too many people.' Leslie wasn't sure she had caught the words right, for immediately after the man had finished speaking, an incredible babble of voices arose, agitated, frightened. She saw the mother with her three children hug the smallest one to her convulsively. As for herself, after the first stunned moment when her chest had contracted with the shock, she felt almost abnormally calm. 'They have weapons,' she murmured calmly. 'How'd they get the guns aboard?

'At a guess, it was one of the ground crew in O'Hare when they cleaned the plane. The guns could have been hidden then, I think,' Scott murmured quietly. He was relaxed after that first strangely dangerous reaction, she noted. 'This has been well planned.'

Well planned. 'It's hard to believe,' she said shakily. The plane began to dip sharply. Leslie studiously kept her eyes away from the window. 'I've never heard of the People's—what were they called?'

'The People's Revolutionary Republic. It's a small group of rebels located south of Florida, north of Cuba. They are on an island and have a military installation there.' He was well informed.

'What or whom are they revolting against?' she asked, gripping the seat tightly as the plane bumped roughly on to the runway. The landing was badly done; presumably the pilot was a bit unnerved too.

'I'm not really sure,' he said calmly, and then noticed her white face. He took her hand, or rather, prised it from the seat arm that she'd been clenching. 'I think it's a combination of declared hatred for the United States, which is not so unusual these days, along with a rejection of the Cuban regime.' The plane taxied slowly and came to a halt some distance from the airport terminals. At a guess, Leslie would say that the hijackers had been in touch with the airport controllers to demand fuel to be sent out to the plane. She took a deep, shaky breath.

'They aren't going to send the fuel,' she said shakily. 'It'll be a stand off.'

'Listen to me, Leslie,' Scott said in a low, urgent voice. 'We're to the back of the plane and chances are that we will be the ones chosen to be held as hostages.' She looked up and about sharply. He was right. They were nearly at the back. 'I want you to get up and move to the empty seat near the front over there. You'll probably be let off, if negotiations allow for the release of the passengers as they'd said. Now, get——'

Horrified, she jerked her hand out of his and stared with huge, hard eyes at him. She looked her accusation before she was able to find the words to speak. 'I think,' she whispered furiously, 'that what you just said is absolutely unspeakable. Look over at the mother with her three children! Count out the seats! Would they all make it off, or would one of them have to stay behind? Would the mother stay, or perhaps the twelve year old? Look,' she gritted between her teeth, 'at the teenage girls just two aisles ahead. Which would have to stay, if I moved up? No, Scott.' She shook her head, her tone contemptuous, her eyes leaping with fury. 'You can move if you like. I'll sit here and take my chances.'

'There is only one seat,' he said, his inflection totally without emotion. 'I had not intended it for myself.' She looked sharply his way, and saw tenseness, the way his eyes burned darkly. He was holding some violent emotion in check.

She asked him shortly, 'Did you really think I would move?' His head turned slowly and he just looked at her. That extreme emotion was gone.

'I didn't know. I'd . . . hoped.'

'You don't know the first thing about me,' she returned tightly, and he was suddenly amused.

'Oh, come now, Les. Surely I know a *little* about you,' he taunted her softly, and her head jerked to the direction of the window.

'How long will it take you to forget what happened that night?' she snapped.

'But, darling, I don't want to forget it, although you seem strangely urgent about forgetting it, yourself. And that is another apparent contradiction about you. If you were the—whore, I believe was your quaint term—you'd have shrugged it off long ago.'

A mistake, she thought. She'd just made a big one. She made herself turn around to smile at him slowly, mockingly. 'Your mistake is thinking I haven't,' she told him amusedly. It was a big effort. 'After all, I'm not the one to keep bringing the subject up.'

It was an accurate thrust and they both knew it. His eyes shuttered. 'Perhaps,' was his only response, and he turned to look straight ahead. Leslie felt limp and exhausted, and the remarkable thing about it, she realised, was that it was from their talk and not from the tense and frightening crisis enacted at the moment.

The cabin was getting hot, uncomfortably so, and over to the right a pretty woman was sobbing quietly into her hands while her husband patted her on the shoulder, looking scared half to death himself. Leslie looked ahead restlessly and then out of the window. Nothing was moving on the runway. The sun shone down, pitilessly bright, white hot yellow, and the grass by the pavement looked scorched and dry. Scott touched her on the arm and nodded ahead. 'It looks like someone else had the same bright idea that I did,' he said quietly. The empty seat he'd spotted was taken. Leslie looked around her. One of the teenage girls was missing.

She said quite without malice, 'I hope she makes it off.' And she was immensely surprised when Scott put his big hand over hers and squeezed briefly before letting go again.

There was a long period of an unusually strange and nerve-racking combination of intense boredom and extreme fear. Leslie could only imagine what kind of negotiations and threats were being issued to the control tower, and her imagination was only too vivid. She'd heard of hijackers threatening to take a passenger each half hour and shooting them until their demands were met. God only knew what was happening in the cockpit and outside. The dark haired man came out periodically, with a machine gun slung over one arm, and he would calmly inspect the passengers. Each time he appeared, there was a profound, fear stricken silence, and everyone collectively sighed with relief when he disappeared again.

'What do you think will happen?' she finally asked, the question bursting from her in a welling of frustration and uncertainty. In contrast, Scott looked merely bored, as his head lay against the back of his seat. She found herself running her eyes over his thick, springy mane of light hair in appreciation, and jerked her thoughts away. How could she be thinking of such irrelevancies, when a tense matter of life or death was hanging in the balance? But even as she thought the silent self-rebuke, she knew she couldn't castigate herself too much. Life or death situations couldn't seem very real, with boredom beginning to overshadow even the fear.

A flurry of activity appeared outside her window and attracted her attention. Scott looked over her shoulder and remarked, 'It looks like something's about to happen. Their demands are being met. That's a fuelling truck.' He pointed, and she nodded without surprise. She knew a sinking in her heart. What would happen now?

'Wait a minute,' she said suddenly. 'Why would they need to refuel? Wasn't this the flight going on to London?'

Scott looked over his shoulder to Jarred and asked him, 'We had a lay-over in New York, didn't we?' At Jarred's nod, he continued, 'They'd needed to refuel anyway, then.'

Leslie was peering out the window, and she suddenly tensed and pointed. 'Look! They're hooking up an exit ramp.' It was moving to the front of the plane. At the far right corner of her window she saw men run back quite some distance and then remain, watching.

'What do you want to bet that those men aren't regular ground crew?' Scott said, grimly amused. She flashed him a look but didn't speak.

Then everything seemed to happen at once, with the dark little attendant opening the hatch and two of the three men coming back with ugly weapons in their hands, bodies tense and eyes alert. 'All right!' the taller man called out sharply.

'I want the people in the first aisle to get their things and get out! You have five seconds, move it!' And they did move fast, their fear making them clumsy, stumbling out in record time. The first class passengers were streaming out from the front, coming out behind the sectioning screen with their eyes dilated and faces showing strain. The dark man continued on down the aisles in this manner, keeping his back to the empty seats and his eyes constantly roving over the remaining passengers. He was nearly to the back and he appeared to be counting heads.

Scott said calmly, 'We aren't going to make it.' She simply nodded her head, not trusting herself to speak. Her shirt was sticking to her back, and she wasn't sure if it was from the heat or her fear. Then nearly everyone was off except for the last several rows, and the armed hijacker was motioning curtly to the young woman who had been quietly crying before. She stared at him dumbly for an instant, and then hesitantly stood. Her husband stood also, only to be met by the dark muzzle of the gun that pointed dead into his chest. The woman erupted into hysterical sobs and started to grab for her husband who, looking none too happy himself, was attempting vainly to push her away. The man grabbed her arm and jerked her back, then pushed her ahead of him while keeping his gun trained on the husband and his eyes roaming the rest of the cabin. At the open hatch another gunman waited, keeping watch on the still world outside, gun cocked and manner tense.

Filled with a consuming anger, Leslie found herself saying quite clearly, 'Why, that filthy bast——' And suddenly she was grabbed and her face pulled into Scott's chest so that she could hardly breathe. His hand was twisted into her hair at the back of her head. She had a brief sensation of breathing in a crisp male scent, a scent that was hauntingly familiar, and she thought, *I know that scent* . . .

Then Scott was hissing in her ear, furiously, 'You fool, keep your mouth shut! Do you want to get yourself or him shot? Can't you see that he wants her to go, to get off the plane?'

She whispered back, her voice muffled against the warm hardness of Scott's shoulder as she pushed vainly with her hands to get away. 'He could have let the husband off, too! What the hell did it matter, if they had twenty-nine hostages, instead of thirty?'

'Oh, God!' he sighed. His hand loosened in her hair, and to her intense shame, she felt a tear trickle out of her eye, and then another. They soaked immediately into his shirt, and she knew that he must have felt it. She felt his hand cup the back of her skull gently, and stroke comfortingly. 'Les, they are setting up a rule of authority. They can't afford to make threats and not carry through with them.'

'I know, I know. Damn it, anyway.' She pushed against his chest and this time he let her up. Then she stared out the window angrily, knuckling at her eyes. When she turned back a few moments later, her face was grim and set. Scott searched her expression and then nodded encouragingly.

The gunman at the hatch had thrown it shut and locked it. The other man backed up the aisle and disappeared. The plane began to whine again, and this time she was nearly sick to her stomach, as the plane turned on the runway, taxied briefly and took off without any further warning. Everything combined had made her nauseous. She closed her eyes, folded her arms across her chest, and grimly concentrated on keeping controlled. This time Scott must have sensed her need for withdrawal, for he left her alone. She didn't see the dark eyes watching her constantly.

After a large slanting curve in the sky, the plane levelled off again and she opened her eyes with a sigh that was more of a groan. Wayne and Jarred were very serious and grim. Jarred looked her way and nodded, with a wink. She couldn't return her usual smile, but she did nod.

Thirty passengers left, a silent, worried group. The young girl had watched her friend disembark and was left alone. There were a few middle-aged couples, the four to them, of course, a few more women and several men, some in their fifties. It was fairly mixed group. She was glad to see that the mother with her three children had got off safely. Leslie loosened her seatbelt and tried to relax. Everyone on the plane had one thing in common: their lives were being changed by today, perhaps fatally, definitely irrevocably. None of them were ever going to be quite the same again.

She had the now very frightening impression that she was being hurtled into a future that she was powerless to prevent.

The flight took forever, it seemed, and yet at the same time, in that queer way when one doesn't want to experience what is ahead, it took hardly any time at all. By now the sun was sinking towards the western sky, and Leslie guessed that it was early evening. She had eaten nothing that day except for some quickly snatched toast that morning and the late morning snack served on the flight to New York, and she was beginning to feel a bit light in the head. After a little bit, the two flight attendants came out with loaded trolleys to serve the thirty passengers supper. When her meal was set in front of her, she looked at it in resignation and disgust. Though she was light-headed, her stomach revolted at the sight of food, a sure sign of nervousness. The other passengers were glumly silent, some shovelling the food in, other just picking listlessly.

'Eat it,' Scott advised her, as he started in on his meal. 'All of it. There's no telling when we'll eat again.'

She hesitated, and then complied, as much as she was able. She'd recognised the wisdom of his advice. She handed him her dessert, though, with a grimace. He took it after a wry glance at her strained face, and demolished it, after eating every scrap on his tray.

After some time, Leslie's ears popped as the plane began to sink once more, and she tightened her seatbelt. All she could see outside was blue water and a rosy clouded sky. 'An island, eh?' she muttered. 'I hope the pilot doesnt miss.'

Their descent became more rapid, and if Leslie thought a normal landing was bad enough, she found the experience of dropping out of the sky to apparently nothing but ocean, utterly terrifying. She abandoned all pride and burrowed into Scott's ready shoulder while he held her tightly with one arm, murmuring into her hair. The plane bumped, and when Leslie emerged, she was looked out to a small asphalt runway bordered with a green profusion of tangled plant life. Off in the distance she saw several low constructed buildings. A gunman, the one who had kept watch out the hatch while the passengers had disembarked, came down the aisle, flicking his gaze over everyone in the group. She had the impression that he didn't miss much. Then he told everybody to gather their belongings and prepare to exit the plane. While he spoke, the plane eased to a halt and the hatch was opened by the taller gunman.

They motioned and the passengers reluctantly exited, forced to go down a ladder. Leslie, loath to toss her bag to the ground and risk breaking her recorder, slung it on to her shoulder awkwardly and prepared to climb down, but she was stopped by Scott's hand on the shoulder strap, detaining her.

He looked extremely patient. 'I don't think that any of them would particularly care if you were to break a leg or not. You'd have to fend for yourself,

I'd make a bet, and I don't relish being the one to have to care for you. You'd better give me that.'

Annoyed, she jerked away. 'No! I'll handle it, myself. No one's asked for your help.' And she turned and would have started down the ladder, but for his adroit plucking away of her bag and slinging it to his shoulder stubbornly. She might have stayed to argue, but one of the hijackers, attracted by the delay, headed their way with a frown so she nimbly slipped down without anything more to say. He was right behind her, and his feet had barely touched the ground before she took her bag again, ignoring his exaggerated, 'You're welcome.'

As soon as Jarred and Wayne had descended, they unobtrusively made their way to stand by Leslie and Scott as all of the passengers huddled in an apprehensive bunch.

Wayne asked her lowly out of the side of his mouth, 'Where the hell are we—Cuba?'

She whispered back, 'I've no idea, but from the sounds of things, with this group Cuba's the last place we would be.'

They both fell silent as several men from the cluster of buildings approached the group, two slightly ahead of the others and the older man definitely a person of authority. They walked up to the three hijackers, the last two men coming down after the captain and his crew had disembarked. The flight attendants were huddled together, except for the one that Leslie had noted earlier.

She was with the hijackers. The group looked to the hostages and talked in low voices.

Wayne looked into the sun, squinting at the evening's ray. The heat was already at work on Leslie's back, drenching her in wetness. 'Can you make out what they're saying?' he asked her conversationally.

She turned her head so that the men couldn't see her lips. 'Too far, but I think they're speaking Spanish.'

Wayne nodded while Scott asked her, 'You speak Spanish too?' She caught one of the men looking their way, so she contented herself with a slight nod.

Then the group of armed men marched their way, motioning for the group to walk to the cluster of buildings. On the way, Scott said lowly, 'Try not to get separated.' Then they were herded into one of the buildings and ordered to surrender their belongings for a search. Several of the men came forward and without further conversation began to take bags and rifle through them. Everything was brought out and examined, even personal items, which caused much embarrassment for some of the women passengers. Leslie's bag was taken from her nerveless fingers and dumped on to the table. Her recorder was brought out and promptly smashed on to the floor, destroyed beyond repair. At that she cried out in protest, but the man searching her things had found her press pass and was looking her over with piercing eyes. He walked over to the man who appeared to be in

charge, and he in turn came over to look her over
and her belongings with an expressionless face. He
motioned, and her searcher came up behind her to
take hold of her arm, none too gently. Again she
cried out, this time in fear, and she twisted around
to look for Scott and the others, who were right
beside her.

Scott came forward with a murderous expression
on his face, only to jerk to a halt as a muzzle of a
rifle was pointed into his midsection. 'Cut it out,
she hasn't done——' he began angrily. The man
holding Leslie's arm started to drag her away, and
at that, Scott started convulsively forward, gun or
no gun, this time to be held by both Jarred and
Wayne, to keep him from being shot. The last
thing that Leslie saw before she was yanked out of
the room and into a hall was of him fighting
Wayne and Jarred, his face a mask of fury.

She was marched along the corridor until they
came to a door which the man opened and thrust
her through. There was little in the room
beyond—a table, a few chairs, a window with a
crude curtain hanging in front of it, and an ash
tray. Then the man shut the door behind him,
leaned against the wall and waited. Leslie, after
looking around her for a few moments, gingerly
eased herself into a chair and waited too,
wondering miserably what she was waiting for.

She hadn't long to wonder. Soon the man in
charge came in. He was dressed just like all the
others, in regulation khaki pants, plain cotton
shirt, and of course the weapons. He seemed in his

late thirties, she mused, maybe early forties. His eyes were cold. He sat down across from her and began to fire questions at her. Was she travelling alone? With whom was she travelling? What was her destination? Was she on assignment, and if so, what was her assignment? Suspecting that the other three would be subjected to the same kind of questioning, and having no reason to lie, Leslie told him the truth as much as she was able to, sometimes stumbling because she didn't understand the reasoning behind the questions. And all through it all, she was subjected to the man's roaming, speculative gaze which made her more nervous than anything else. Why was she, an unmarried woman, travelling with three men and going to foreign countries? The implication was obvious, and it angered her.

After asking her every conceivable question that he could think of, he then started over again, and the minutes slowly ticked into an hour, then two, then three. She realised that she was given more harassment just because she was a woman and a member of the press, but it didn't make her patience wear any better.

'It appears that there is a possibility that you have been sent to spy on the People's Revolutionary Republic of Cuba,' he told her expressionlessly, his eyes flicking over her once again. Tired and irritable, she leaned her head on one hand, wondering fleetingly if she was ever going to get through this.

'That is utter nonsense and you know it,' she

retorted flatly, too angry and exhausted to care.
'How could we have been sent for that reason
when our flights weren't scheduled anywhere near
Cuba or Florida, and there's no way we could
have known about the hijacking?'

'Insolence will make things harder for you.'

'You are going to do what you wish anyway; my
attitude is not about to change that. This is sheer
harassment.'

'What was your intended destination?'

'Why the hell are you asking me that again?
Check my damned ticket! You've asked me that
two times already. I'm not about to change my
answer now, even if I were lying?'

'With whom are you travelling?'

'I've told you!'

'Which newspaper do you work for?'

Her voice now completely flat, and yet somehow
filled with suppressed fury, she said tightly, 'I want
to speak to your commanding officer.'

The man stood. 'You are speaking to him.' He
got out of his chair and went to the door, opened
it, and nodded to the man who had remained as a
guard. The man came in, took Leslie's arm, and
marched her back down the hall. She walked
along, having to hurry to keep up with the man's
longer strides, wondering miserably where she
was being taken this time. But instead of taking
her somewhere unknown, which had been her fear,
he took her back the way they'd come, opened the
door to the large room and thrust her inside.

She was left to walk the rest of the way into the

room, where everyone was still kept, she saw, and she eagerly searched the group for the men. They were standing a little off to the side, clustered close together, talking in low tones and looking worried. At the sound of the door opening and the sight of her entrance, they looked immeasurably relieved, and Scott came forward to take her shoulders in a bruising grip.

Looking down into her face, he rasped, 'Are you all right, for God's sake?'

She vaguely noticed the others coming up around her, all three looking as tired and as drawn as she felt. She nodded, smiling as best as she could to reassure. 'I'm fine, honestly.'

His grim expression didn't ease. 'They didn't hurt you in any way, did they?'

'No. No, really, they didn't. A man took me to a small room, and another man came in and asked me a lot of questions over and over. It was really nothing but harassment, and a sexual one at that.' Unable to stop himself, she put her hands up and covered Scott's, squeezing lightly. His hands then fell away.

Wayne told her, 'As soon as they found our press passes, we all were taken into separate rooms and interrogated. No doubt they will check answers to see if any of us has lied. But we were brought back some time ago, and as you were the first to be taken out and weren't back yet, we started to get really worried.' His puckish face still looked strained, and Leslie patted him affectionately on the cheek. For some reason she then glanced briefly over to Scott and stiffened in surprise and puzzlement when she saw his face tighten, then become expressionless.

Jarred remarked, 'Do you think it was because you were a woman?'

She thought and then nodded slowly. 'That, and I also had the tape recorder, remember. Maybe they were afraid they'd been taped.' Wayne dropped his hand to her shoulder and she smiled at him in thanks for his support.

She then went over to where her bag had been left, clucking in dismay over the broken remains of her recorder and the ripped out decks of blank tape. She gathered everything that was undamaged together and stuffed it back into her bag, looking over the group as she did so. Everyone was looking haggard and drawn, and quite definitely the worse for wear, and when she counted heads, she found a few people missing. Presumably for one reason or another, some of the others were being questioned also.

Feeling limp and bedraggled, she looked around the large, ugly room. There were only a few long tables and no chairs, so she went over to one side with her back against the wall and slid down to sit, leaning her head dejectedly back. Wayne was standing with his back to her, running his hands through his hair and scratching. Jarred had started to pace back and forth, his actions like a caged, impatient animal, and Scott was aloof from all the rest, hands in his pockets, head thrown back as he stared up at the ceiling in an attitude of thought.

Leslie marvelled that of the three men, all of whom were attractive males in their own right, Scott should be the one to stand out. It wasn't his looks necessarily, though his nearly white hair against such dark skin was different enough, but there was a certain air about him. It was something in the set to his solid, bulky shoulders, the cocked angle of his head, the commanding expression in his eyes. She ran her eyes down his entire length, down the curve of his back to the angle of his hips and long line of his legs, surprising in herself another flush of sexual awareness. At this, she jerked her head away and studied the rest of the group, angry with her apparent fixation with a man she no longer wanted to be involved with. It wasn't enough that she had to make a fool of herself after four fairly placid years, but instead of being assuaged by that one night of indiscretion, she'd found her body's memories awakened. Whatever else had gone wrong in her relationship with Dennis, the sex had always been good. She ground her teeth, and looked the people over for signs of stress.

They were there in abundance. Although none of the women happened to be crying, several looked as if they'd like to or already had, and everyone was worn down, exhausted. The captain and the flight crew were together. That made Leslie think of the small attendant who was the apparent link with the hijackers, and thought that if she ever came face to face with the girl, she could quite cheerfully give her a slapping.

After a long period of more boredom and anxiety, the rest of the group was let back into the room, and then things started to happen. Several armed men came into the room and motioned for the group to head on outside, which everyone did, gathering their bags and stumbling tiredly out into the evening. As Leslie left the building, she found that Wayne, Jarred and Scott had come together around her, instinctively protective, attempting to stay with each other if possible. It gave her a warm glow of comfort inside, and she couldn't help smiling a little, in spite of the situation. They were led past several buildings, to one that stood somewhat apart from the others. It was rather small and as ugly as the others. They were herded in to find that it was a barracks of sorts, with cots lined up against the walls and at the other end small bathrooms with the bare minimum of facilities. There were no windows in the bathrooms, and the ones in the larger room could not be opened in any way. There were no explanations, no reassurances of their safety, no estimations as to their stay. The guards simply left after marching everyone in, and the double doors were slammed and locked.

After the most brief of inspections, everyone found that there were not even enough cots to go around. And so, tired, hungry, dispirited and irritable, the group was left to fend for themselves for the night. Leslie didn't even attempt to get herself a cot, but instead threw down her bag and then threw herself down too, much too exhausted, anxious only to end a day that had the distinction of being, aside from the day when she'd found out that her family was dead, the worst day of her life.

CHAPTER FOUR

AFTER one of the most miserable days in her life, Leslie proceeded to spend one of the most miserable nights in her life on the hard floor of the barrack. There was simply no way to get comfortable: after tentatively tossing and turning for a few hours, she was forced to lie flat on her back, or otherwise bruise her hips by laying on her side. She did manage to doze towards morning, though only fitfully.

As a consequence, she was one of the first up the next morning, already washed and dressed in fresh clothes by the time most of the others were beginning to stir. There were no cheerful good morning greetings. Everyone more or less groaned in resignation as they opened their eyes and found the whole nightmare a reality and not a dream. Sitting on a now vacant cot, Leslie combed out her hair and then tied it back with a blue ribbon. She was curled up at one end of the bed, using her canvas bag as a back rest when Scott came up and eased himself down beside her. She spared a flick of her eyes for him, briefly noting his own change of attire, and then she looked back to the rest of the group, making a mental note of the people already to the point of bickering. She would take care to steer clear of them, having no desire to waste her energy in such useless scenes.

'Nice people,' Scott murmured, his own head tilted back, eyes hard and amused.

'But I wouldn't want to live with them,' she finished, grinning wryly. 'It's amazing just how many of them remind me of people from my home town, some of them my relatives.'

'And where is your home town?' He turned his head as he leaned back on both hands, but she wasn't paying attention, her eyes already focused on something he couldn't see.

'It's a small town in southern Illinois. The name isn't important. Most people in the world haven't been there, and most will never be going there. I expect it's a bit like any other small town in the Midwest. Funny how a small place can have such a representative of personality types that you can find anywhere.'

'Visit there much?' The question was nonchalant. She was therefore unprepared for the keen, assessing gaze that was trained on her, when she happened to casually glance his way. He was quite seriously paying attention to her.

'As seldom as possible,' she said shortly. 'Funerals and weddings, and only then until I can manage to slip away quietly. They all stifle me to death.'

'The whole town?' he murmured laughingly, and she had to smile.

'Of course not. I guess I'm only talking about my family right now.' She grinned mirthlessly.

'They will have a fit when they find out about all this. It will, naturally, have been all my fault for stubbornly pursuing my choice of career. Sooner or later, something like this was bound to happen. After this, maybe I'll have enough sense to settle down, like any other normal young woman, and stop traipsing off into God-only-knows-what-kind-of-country. End of lecture.'

He was laughing by the end of her dry little speech, and her own grin widened to contain amusement as she cocked a rueful brow his way. 'You are being serious?'

'But, of course.'

Just at that moment, the door opened to reveal two men carrying in large trays laden with fruit and bread, and what was hopefully coffee steaming from two heavy pots. They set down the food and turned to depart, but were forestalled by the captain, who asked them if it were possible to get the passengers' luggage from the plane. He soon found his enquiry to be in vain, however, as it became apparent that neither of the two men could speak English. Leslie watched in silence and sensed the presence of someone just behind her. She turned and found both Wayne and Jarred squatting on the other side of Scott, listening to the frustrating exchange like everyone else.

Wayne asked her in a low voice, 'Are you going to offer to help?'

She frowned and would have replied, but Scott spoke for her. 'It might be to our advantage if they thought no one here could speak Spanish. Then we

might be able to overhear something of value.'
He'd spoken in a low whisper to avoid being
overheard himself, and Leslie looked around him to
Wayne for confirmation. He was nodding in
agreement, so she kept silent.

Finally the captain managed to convey to one of
the men that he wanted to talk to someone in
charge. The man curtly nodded, and then they
both left, locking the door securely behind them.
Some time later the door opened again, and the
man who had questioned Leslie was standing there
impassively, looking over the group with an
expressionless face. Everyone had abruptly stood
at his entrance, and the captain came forward
again with his request. Leslie, who happened to be
on the other side of the room, felt no desire to get
any closer to the exchange and thus draw attention
to herself, and so she missed much of what was
said. It did her no good to try to remain
unobtrusive, though, for the man's eyes wandered
over the group until he came to her. He then
looked her over with a gaze that made her
extremely nervous. She forced herself to look cool
and even faintly insolent as she stared back. Scott
moved restlessly beside her. The man then looked
away and nodded curtly to the captain and said
something else. Then he walked out. There was a
general bustle and the men seemed to be preparing
to go somewhere. Leslie asked Jarred, who walked
back to her and Scott, 'What is going on?'

'The men are going to get the luggage off the
plane while a few soldiers stand guard,' was his

reply. 'The commander said basically that if we want the luggage so badly, we can get it ourselves. He said he couldn't spare the men for something so unproductive.'

She shrugged. 'Well, I guess that's fair enough. At least it will give you fellows something to do, which is more than I can say for myself. If we're cooped up like this for very long, I promise, I shall go quite mad at the first opportunity.' He grinned at her sympathetically, and then the door was opened again. The men were ushered out.

Left on their own, the women milled around rather aimlessly until Leslie couldn't stand the sight of the untidy cots and started to straighten them up, moving briskly. Gradually she became aware that the others were pitching in also and talking in voices that betrayed their nervousness. The young teenager was helping too. In fact, the only woman who was not paying attention to what was happening in the room was a middle-aged woman who stared out the window and smoked incessantly. Leslie counted up the women and noted that there were actually fewer women than men; there were only eleven in the group right at the moment. An uneven number. Having filed away this piece of trivia, she then proceeded to study each one in turn and detail. She introduced herself to the young woman helping her with one of the beds, and the other woman responded in a friendly manner. Soon almost everyone was gathering around, eager to talk. The woman, watching out the window and smoking, did not come over. Leslie then realised that she was one of the married women and no doubt was anxiously awaiting the return of her husband. She had a strained look on her face, and a tightness around her eyes and mouth. Her eyes darted all over the place restlessly, and she couldn't seem to keep her hands still. As Leslie talked with the others, listening with only half her attention to what was said, she studied the older woman rather worriedly. The unmistakable signs of stress were there; if anyone were to break under the pressures of their unexpected ordeal, she feared it would be this one. She turned her attention back to the group.

Pat, the teenager, was fresh faced and healthy looking rather than strictly pretty, though she did have a nice figure. She was indomitably cheerful, a natural state of being, Leslie concluded, and not a release of nervous tension. The young woman to whom Leslie first introduced herself, Sherri, was in her early twenties and rather shy. These were the two that Leslie felt most attracted to, and the ones who seemed the most interested in herself. Another woman in her thirties named Helen looked rather cold, though strikingly beautiful, and though she listened to the other's conversation, she did not offer much about herself. The two flight attendants—Leslie didn't know what happened to the dark haired woman and didn't much care—stayed pretty much close together and seemed to be good friends, though they were talkative enough with the rest of the women. The last three were married and also showing signs of anxiety as time went by.

After a while, when Leslie had begun to feel rather edgy herself, unmistakable sounds of people approaching had everyone jumping to their feet in hope and apprehension. The door swung open, bright sunlight spilling into the shadowed interior, and the men filed in, loaded down with suitcases and overnight bags, and canvas duffle bags. All of the women sighed in collective relief, and the married couples rushed to their spouses. Leslie looked for her friends, relaxing and smiling at them when she caught sight of the three. The guards locked the door behind the last of the men, and the group was left to themselves once more.

Leslie walked up and took her bag from Wayne with a thanks, asking, 'Did you have any trouble getting the luggage? Were the guards polite or threatening?' She looked over to Scott quickly as she asked her questions, her eyes showing her relief. He walked over and dropped his hand to her shoulder for brief reassurance.

'Which question first?' Wayne queried, giving her a lopsided grin. 'Yes, we had a bit of trouble getting all of the luggage because we had to go through the whole load to get it all. And the guards weren't really anything except there. Of course, none of us tried to make a break for it.'

Scott remarked, 'They were watchful, but it wasn't anything that was particularly nerve-racking.' She nodded.

After some bustle, things more or less settled down, and soon Leslie was nearly out of her mind with the boredom. She rummaged in her things and drew out her stationery, preparing to try a bit of writing. Soon, however, she found that she just couldn't settle into anything and she threw down her pad and pen in disgust. Scott lounged nearby and grinned at her sympathetically. His blond hair was casually rumpled, and in the heat of the day he had his shirt unbuttoned to his waist, a luxury, she thought wistfully, that she wished she could indulge. With the air of a magician producing a rabbit out of a hat, he flourished a pack of playing cards, well used, under her surprised and then delighted nose.

'Do you know how to play poker?' he asked her, shuffling deftly. She shook her head, fascinated with the fluid movements of his fingers. 'Well, then, I guess I'll have to teach you.' He motioned her to a corner, and they sat cross-legged on the floor. He dealt, while explaining the basic rules to her, and then laid out his cards, telling her to do the same. She laughed at him while clutching the cards to her chest.

'Oh, no you don't!' she declared. 'One thing I do know about poker is that you don't let the opponent know your hand!' Cautiously she peered at her cards, keeping them close to her body and eyeing him suspiciously over the edge while he shook with amusement. Her brow cocked, her lips pursed, and she rearranged her hand thoughtfully, aware of his laughter, and his exaggeratedly patient regard. Then she laid down her three of a kind and picked up a card from the stack by his thigh. 'Your turn.'

'That's rummy!' he accused.

'That's right!' She wrinkled her nose and childishly crossed her eyes.

'You've seen my cards. We'll have to deal over if we're going to play that.' He captured her hands and tried to take her cards away from her.

She howled at him and struggled futilely to hold on to her hand without bending or ruining the cards. He was soon victorious, and as soon as she lost the hold on her cards, she grabbed up the rest of the deck, aimed it for his face, bent them in an arc and shot them at him in a rapid fire succession. Laughing, he tried to catch them all, but it was dismally hopeless. He sat in a puddle of scattered cards while she stood and laughed down at him. As he watched, her eyes suddenly widened as she stared down, and then the vivid amusement and enjoyment shuttered into a blank mask. Her fine features, in contrast to the vivaciousness of a moment before, were almost dull.

He leaned back on one hand and stared up at her thoughtfully. 'Sit down,' he said quietly.

Her eyes slid away. 'No, I think I'm going to——'

He interrupted as quietly, but she found herself shutting her mouth immediately in deference to his words. 'I said sit down,' he repeated softly, eyes steady. 'And if you don't do it, I'll make you. We've attracted enough attention to ourselves already. You wouldn't want me to make you, would you?'

She glanced swiftly around and found eyes

interestedly trained on their play. Taking a deep breath, she sat and faced him stiffly. He started to stack up the cards carefully, one by one, and by his very care, she knew he wasn't paying attention to it. 'I get this feeling whenever I'm around you,' he said reflectively, deep voice nearly a rumble. Involuntarily she glanced at his chest and found herself drawn, in spite of herself, to the brown, silken skin. Her head tilted up and she stared at the ceiling. 'I see glimpses of a Leslie whom I admire and am attracted to, but whenever she sees me coming, she slams a door in my face so fast and so hard that it makes my head spin. Why is that? What does that Leslie have to hide?'

'Your last statement is a presumption,' she returned, feeling oddly breathless. She sucked in air deeply, held it a moment, and then continued, 'You are going on the assumption that first of all I have something to hide, and secondly, that I would for some reason feel the need to hide it from you, of all people. You have no power over me to make me afraid of what I do, or do not, tell you about myself.'

'Is that what you're afraid of? Are you afraid of letting me glimpse perhaps too much of you, a certain something that would give me some kind of hold over you? What a strange preoccupation you have! How have I ever threatened you, or encroached on your privacy?'

She just looked at him, unable to reply. Then she pushed off the floor and walked to the window, feeling constricted. She stood there and stared out at the lush, green, alien growth of the forest near by, so confused she couldn't answer the questions she tentatively asked herself. Shame, fear, and resentment teemed in her in a jumble, along with a certain amount of pride, and strangely, loneliness.

As the afternoon crept by, agonisingly slowly, into early evening, almost everyone in the barrack was ready to climb the walls in supreme frustration. Uncertainty, boredom, tension, fear, anxiety, all made the people cooped up together snappish, hemmed in, rude. Finally she was to the point where she had just about had enough, unable to stand the sight of the others pacing around and sick to death of the spare, ugly building. Leslie marched on over to the door and rapped sharply. There was no answer, so she rapped again, harder. Silence fell in the room behind her as people turned to look, curiously.

'What is she doing?' a woman's voice querulously demanded. Leslie didn't turn her head, identifying the voice as the nervous older lady.

Finally someone came and a lock scraped at the door. Leslie stepped back and let the door swing open. Something made her glance briefly to her right. Scott stood not far away, watching alertly. Jarred and Wayne were just behind him, a silent, though puzzled support. She flashed them a grateful look.

One of the guards stuck in his head and said in short, impatient sounding Spanish, 'What the hell do you want?' But Leslie looked at him blankly, and then pushed right past him to march into the sunlight. She heard gasps behind her, exclamations, and then the other guard snapped up his gun to point it into her stomach. Acting far more bravely than she felt, she put her hands on her hips and glared at him. He told her to move back into the building before he blew her into little pieces. She didn't blink an eye, sure that he thought she couldn't understand, and told him to go to blazes. He glared at her and asked the other guard what he should do. The other man, barricading the open doorway and training his gun on the occupants inside, shrugged.

The commotion caught the attention of some men moving around at the other buildings, and soon the commander was striding impatiently their way, anger taut in every body line. He approached Leslie, who refused to shrink away, though her insides were like jelly, quivering. 'What is the meaning of this?' he asked harshly.

She threw back her head and was haughty. 'I am not an animal, sir, nor am I used to being cooped up like a chicken.'

He cocked a sardonic eyebrow. 'Come now, surely you are much more pretty than a chicken,' he murmured mockingly. In spite of herself, her mouth quirked.

'Your guards have machine guns,' she stated, with a wide gesture of one hand.

He looked his two men over. 'To the best of my knowledge, yes.' She was relieved to see that instead of staying angry, he now appeared more amused and entertained.

She continued, 'My understanding of such weaponry is not good, but presumably the guns can fire at least eight rounds per second?'

'As an estimation, it is good enough.' His eyes were hooded; she couldn't tell what he was thinking, but at least he was letting her finish.

'Then with two guards shooting, at sixteen rounds per second, and with thirty people, you should have us all shot within five seconds, max..' she concluded flatly.

'Assuredly, if that were my intention.'

'Not even the fastest professional runner could make it to the treeline over there in less than eight to ten seconds, therefore it is not logically possible for any of us to escape. And where would we go, anyway, on an island?' Dead silence, in front of her and behind. 'Then why, may I ask you, are we kept shut in that horrible closed-in building all day without the least chance to stretch our legs? Surely even your men cannot be afraid of us, unarmed and defenceless as we are. If they were positioned far enough away, they could easily shoot down anyone who tried to come too close, or who tried to run. In short, sir,' and she suddenly grinned at him, blue eyes sparkling, 'I would like some fresh air, please.'

He regarded her for a moment or two in inscrutable silence. One of the guards said something extremely rude. Her expression never flickered. Then with a short laugh the commander fired rapid Spanish to the two guards, telling them to set up markers in the wide clearing. Leslie forced herself to look slightly puzzled, exaggeratedly patient, arms crossed, mouth pursed. The borders were marked, a good thirty paces in length, with what looked like paint cans. He then turned and flicked his eyes suggestively over Leslie's figure. 'None of you may go beyond these borders. If you even attempt it you will be instantly shot. If there is any trouble at all caused by this, you will be sent back inside to remain there. Abuse this privilege in any way and you will lose it forever. You cannot remain out after sunset.' And without another glance, he turned on his heel and left.

The tension melted away, and everyone laughed a little in relief. There was a general exodus to the open space, where people made themselves comfortable in the long cushiony grass, walked around for exercise, and talked. Leslie flopped down and spread her arms over her head as she stretched out her legs, laughing at something Pat said. A dark shadow blocked out the slanting evening rays and Scott sat down beside her.

'Quite a scene you caused,' he remarked mildly, shading his eyes and staring to the cluster of buildings some distance away.

'Nothing ventured, nothing gained,' was her flippant reply.

He turned his head sharply and stared at her hard. 'But was that quite the way to go about it?' he asked calmly. 'I'm not ashamed to admit that it gave me a queasy feeling to see the muzzle of that gun pointed dead at your delectable abdomen. Why'd you do it?'

'It wasn't really such a gamble,' she said, closing her eyes and basking in the sun's warmth. 'I was no obvious threat to the guards, and so they would not have wanted to be responsible for injuring or killing me. The commander was the one last night who interrogated me, and underneath the harassment he was attracted to me. He—gives me looks that . . .' She didn't finish the sentence, but shuddered.

Scott's eyes, as they looked again towards the buildings, were hard. 'I know.'

'Well, then, I did what any female would have done. I captured his attention, amused him, while asking for something that was really very reasonable, and because he was diverted, and because I batted my baby blues at him——' She fluttered her eyelashes at Scott, who laughed. '—he said yes. It was just a little manipulation.'

'A universally feminine trait, eh? No, don't look at me that way! I quite agree with you. All one has to do is look back at history to realise that more often than not the woman has been placed in positions of vulnerablility. You do what you can to survive, that's all.'

'Exactly.' She abruptly sat up and plucked at the grass restlessly. She thought of how she had cajoled Dennis into letting her enrol for a few college courses, to keep herself from going crazy. Her mouth twisted as she felt shame deep within her. She shouldn't have had to beg. But she had given him that power over herself, and it is always harder to take power than to give it away. She had no one but herself to blame. Sensing eyes on her, she looked up and encountered Scott's dark, oddly sympathetic eyes, as if he knew what she had been thinking. She grimaced, eyes falling away. 'And for what was gained, it was well worth it,' she continued, oddly defensive. 'We've got more freedom, fresh air and some space . . .'

'. . . and a good view of the buildings over there, so that we can see what is going on,' he finished, looking at her instead of the buildings.

'You—you aren't thinking of trying anything, are you?' she whispered, eyes wide.

'Who can tell? I certainly don't plan on doing anything foolish, but then circumstances are a bit beyond my power of control,' he replied off-handedly, glancing sharply at either guard to make sure they were well away. 'By the way——'

'By the way, what?' Wayne asked, as he and Jarred walked up to squat beside them. He was regarded with a sharp look from Scott.

'Keep your voices down,' Scott admonished him softly. 'I was just thinking that there's every chance that our guards have been instructed to pretend they don't know English, just as we're pretending, and for the same reasons. What better way to keep an eye on the hostages?'

Silence for a moment. Leslie felt a chill run down her spine. Jarred looked thoughtful, and Wayne looked uncomfortable. 'Wow. It's not so much what you've already said,' she muttered, 'but the thought of what you could have said.'

Wayne flashed her a look and Jarred nodded. 'It makes sense,' he said. 'All the same, it's an eerie feeling, isn't it, Les?'

Wayne said abruptly, 'What in the world do you think they want from us, anyway? The whole situation doesn't add up.'

'No, it doesn't,' agreed Scott slowly, turning back from squinting at the sinking sun. Jarred and he exchanged a look. Leslie stirred in the grass beside him. She felt oddly reassured by the sheer bulk of the man sitting by her. It was irrational, she knew, for at the moment Scott was as vulnerable as the others. But the intellectual knowledge didn't make the feeling go away. Whereas everyone else reacted with various disconcerted emotions: fear, anxiety, resentment— Scott acted more like a cat who lands on its feet, cool and collected, always storing up information and always observing. While being in a position of uncontrol, he gave the impression of having everything well in hand. It was soothing.

Covering up her true feeling, she asked, 'What d'you mean?'

'None of it adds up,' Wayne replied, turning around and facing the forest, away from the alert guards. Scott and Jarred were watching him alertly, keenly. Scott leaned back on his elbows as his shirt fell open, his nearly white hair glinting in the light, shadowing dark face and eyes. 'Why would the People's Revolutionary Republic want

to hijack an American airliner and risk the
retribution of the admittedly powerful U.S.
government? They're a small enough group and
already in an uncomfortable situation with Cuba
so close by and hostile. Their island is sandwiched
right between the two powers. If their politics
would have allowed it, they would have been wise
to embrace capitalism and the States, but they're
as communist as Cuba, right? Their main gripe is
that they don't like the present Cuban government.'

'They had help from someone who worked on
the airline,' Leslie murmured thoughtfully. 'A
logical explanation would be that they needed
someone or something out of the States badly
enough to hijack a plane in order to do it.'

She looked around. Scott's face was about as
readable as a blank rock. Jarred was plucking
grass, head bent. Wayne was the one who
answered, 'That's a fair guess. But then the
question is what or whom?'

After a bit of useless speculation and half
hearted discussion, during which both Scott and
Jarred were silent, Leslie stood and restlessly
walked around the designated area. Scott was
moodily preoccupied, staring at the forest and
running a blade of grass through his long fingers.
Wayne and Jarred seemed as disinclined to talk.
She walked towards the building and then turned
to walk to the other border. As she did this a
second time, she noticed the commander coming
towards the guard closest to her. She curled up

into the grass, her back half turned to him, plucking the green strands idly.

He must have come up right beside the guard, for he said quite audibly, in Spanish, 'It won't be long, now.'

Leslie pricked up her ears, striving to act supremely unconcerned and unknowing. Though the two men were standing about ten paces away, she could hear them fairly clearly. If there had been the slightest breeze, she wouldn't have been able to, but as luck would have it, the air was as still as could be. A bee droned by.

The guard said, 'It's been too long already. I don't like it . . .'

'It couldn't be helped. We're waiting right now to hear from our contacts. The news team and a few others could be working undercover. Nearly everyone else checks out.'

'Sh, one of them is right over there.' Leslie knew that it was her they were talking about.

'Don't worry. She doesn't know Spanish,' the commander said. 'Her face was totally blank when you so graphically interrupted earlier. We can't get anything on the reporters, or a few of the men. There's no telling how much Rodriquez let out before we caught up with him. We may just have to kill them before we relocate.'

Leslie turned her head and stared blindly out to the forest, her face chalk white, as shock rippled through her. Her eyes flickered to Scott, Wayne and Jarred. Wayne glanced her way, and then glanced again, his attention arrested by her pallor which was obvious even from that distance. Then he deliberately and casually turned away, saying something to the other two. After a moment, they glanced her way briefly, uninterestedly.

The guard was muttering something.

The commander replied, '. . . know that he had to have told them something . . . flights to Cuba were being watched. It's been . . .' The wind was beginning to gust his words away. Leslie crushed a blade of grass. '. . . still very profitable. Florida's become too risky, anyway. Too many patrols.'

What did he mean? She searched her mind for something that made sense. Were they smuggling? He was speaking again so she focused back to the conversation.

'What are we to do?'

The 'commander' said briefly, 'If we don't hear by tomorrow either way, we'll kill the six and move out as soon as possible—before daylight if we have to. Any longer than that and we have to assume that they're on to us and about to make their move. We can't stay. There's too many chances of something going wrong.'

'. . . the last haul, eh?'

'From this location, yes. Have any of them said anything revealing?'

'No, they all sound quite innocent, though the four reporters were pretty tight together for a while and talking about something real low.'

'That's not good.'

'Do you really expect for them to check out that easily? It's only been a day and a half.'

'No, I don't. They haven't enough time. It's a shame. The woman's attractive enough.'

'She's got it in the right places, at least,' the guard agreed appreciatively.

At first Leslie was rooted to the spot, paralysed. But then she stood aimlessly and stretched in a lazy fashion, slow and deliberate, showing off the lines of her body leisurely. Dead silence behind her. Her hands were shaking with a fine tremor, but luckily it wouldn't be distinguished at any distance away.

This was it. The way the cards had fallen was not good, but there was one, slight chance. If she blew it, it wouldn't matter anyway. If she did nothing they would all surely die.

She squinted up at the sun, shaking her hair back from her face so that it fell in a silken tumble down her back. Then she glanced over her shoulder towards the buildings and, incidentally close to where the 'commander' and the guard were standing. Then, as if just becoming aware that he was standing there, Leslie turned her head that much further, looking at him for a long moment from under heavy lids and then smiled her slow smile. Even from ten paces she could see his eyes widen. He walked towards her deliberately, coming to a halt so close beside her, she could feel the heat from his body.

He stared down at her, the message in his eyes unmistakable as they travelled down her length. She felt soiled, dirtied by it, and it took every ounce of effort to hide how repelled she was by him. 'The sun is not too much for you?' he murmured quietly.

Her slow smile widened. She tilted her head to one side. 'It's a bit warm,' she whispered, and brought one hand up to unbutton the top of her blouse, waving an ineffectual hand in the air as if attempting to cool herself down. The opening now exposed the beginnings of the swelling of her breasts and the shadow between. His eyes were drawn to the spot and transfixed by the creamy skin. She drew a deep breath, which heaved her chest, and then blew it out in a sigh. He unconsciously sighed, too. She ran a finger lightly over her skin just below her collarbone. 'I'm all wet with sweat.'

'It's much cooler inside,' he said, and in spite of himself, licked his lips.

She turned guileless eyes to him.'Oh, is it cool in your room? That bunkhouse gets so stuffy, with everyone crammed together like sardines in a can. I'm sure I'll never sleep in there tonight.'

'You would be—more comfortable somewhere else,' he replied, eyes going back to her chest.

She laughed throatily and moved up close to him, standing so near they were almost touching front to front, hands on her hips, head thrown back to expose the line of her graceful throat. His eyes were getting hungry. 'I thought you'd never ask,' she murmured. His gaze snapped to her face and she mockingly cocked an eyebrow at him. 'Why so surprised, commander? If you haven't figured it out by now, you should have. I'm simply a survivor, and I roll with the punches. And I don't like being uncomfortable. You help me ...' Her hand went up and her fingers lightly caressed his jawline, feeling the muscle clench. '. . . and I help you. A most satisfactory arrangement.'

A coldly lustful gleam suffused his eyes, and at that she knew. This was the kind of man who would have no compunction about taking his pleasure with her and then having her shot. It was a good thing she was as intent on using him as he was on using her. He held her eyes as he bent his head forward. She didn't move but again laughed lowly as he nuzzled her neck in front of the entire group. She didn't let herself think or feel, for to think of the awful consequences if she failed or to feel the shame she knew would come, would be disastrous. For one terrible moment she faltered, feeling like she would retch. But then she had herself in complete control, sliding her arms up deliberately to encircle his neck, pulling his mouth to hers.

The shocked silence all around was broken once by a woman's hissing ejaculation, 'Shameless slut!' The man kissing Leslie put his arms around her and hauled her up against him roughly. She let her head fall back. Then the 'commander' was lifting his head to devour her with greedy eyes.

'Come on,' he said thickly, turning and hauling her away with him.

Wayne was fighting mindlessly against the restraining arms that bound him, much in the same way that

Scott had last night. When the haze of fear and rage cleared enough to let him see, he found Jarred and Scott grappling his arms. Some distance away, two guards watched alertly, guns held ready in case of trouble. 'Let go of me,' he snarled, 'or I swear I'll kill you both!'

Scott's face was rock hard, absolutely white, with dark eyes burning blackly with the force of some strong emotion. 'Let it go, Wayne,' he bit out harshly, and even Wayne in the midst of his sick fury stared at the oddness of his intensity. 'It's her life. If she wants to spend it bedding those——'

Wayne swung with everything in his body, and Scott rocked back with the force of the blow to his jaw. Then Wayne found himself flat on his back and seeing the world spin as Scott moved faster than sight and knocked him clean off the ground.

He just lay there, nursing his jaw, saying hopelessly, 'You bastard. Don't you ever say filthy things about Leslie again, do you hear? She wouldn't do that! My God, she's the most celibate woman I've ever met! She's been that way ever since her husband and daughter died, four years ago!'

Scott blanched. 'Husband?'

'Yes! You fool, don't you realise——' Wayne was shouting it out and Jarred grabbed his arm to gesture silence with his hand, out of the two guards' line of sight. He continued more quietly, nearly in tears now and unashamed of it. 'Don't you realise what happened? She overheard something, something that's frightened her so badly, she's about to do something desperate! I don't know what she'll try, but she's going to try something! When she was first hired, Carl made her take self-defence courses so that she could take care of herself in a rough situation, in case I wasn't around to help her.' Wayne nodded to the buildings behind him, whispering, 'There are too many of them. They are all over the place.' Jarred and Scott looked totally blank, stunned. He finished miserably, 'You know what's going to happen, don't you? She's going to get herself killed.'

CHAPTER FIVE

'WHAT'S your name?' Leslie asked, with a great effort managing to sound nonchalant.'

'Call me Paul.' She nodded, and he ushered her into a sparsely furnished bedroom. She sent a swift glance around; the room was not especially clean, but at least there was a fair chance that there were no little animals living under the bed. A wave of pure panic shocked through her. She clamped it down. One chance only.

She walked further into the room carelessly, and his grasping, hurting hands came to her upper arms. But she forestalled him, putting a light finger to his lips and smiling provocatively up into his lustful eyes.

She then stepped back, her eyes holding him, promising things she dared not contemplate. For one horrible moment she thought that he would not let her go, but he did. She moved over to the door and found a lock, turning it, glancing coyly back over her shoulder. Her move made his eyebrows shoot up, and then he looked amused, but his look of amusement didn't last for long. She started to walk forward very slowly, her fingers going to her blouse. His eyes were arrested by the movement, and he flushed with excitement. He would have come forward then, but she shook her head, moving her tongue over her lips. She could feel his desire barely held in check, and she knew that her time was running out. Soon she would no longer be able to keep him away.

'Take your time,' she murmured lowly. She walked over to the bed, holding his gaze, and his eyes were then dropping to her chest and staying there. 'We have all the time in the world.' She eased back on the bed, deliberately slipped off a shoe and let it plop, leaning back on one hand and smiling at him suggestively. Only one chance . . .

Because of the heat of the day, she hadn't put on a bra, and as her blouse fell open bit by bit, she felt a moment of secret exultation. It was the deciding factor; she had him completely now. He ripped off his shirt and threw it into a corner, and then unzipped and drew down his pants, his eyes hot on her, making her want to writhe in disgust. Her eyes beckoned, her smile invited, and her hand drew her shirt slowly apart the rest of the way as she casually propped one foot on the bed, the other leg thrown out. Her breathing was coming heavier as excitement, fear, revulsion—all caused the adrenalin to surge. He saw it, mistook it for passion, and then he came for her.

He never noticed that the foot she had propped on the bed was the one fully shod. All of his attention was on her bare chest, her parted lips, the movement of her chest as her breathing deepened.

He never saw the kick that levelled him, knocked him clean out.

Leslie jerked to her feet as the commander arced back to the wall behind him and slumped to the floor. She pulled her shirt together with a violent movement and buttoned it with jerky fingers that bespoke of disgust and total revulsion. Then she went over to Paul and poked him gingerly with her foot. He didn't budge. She bent down and gave a great heave, and his body flopped over like a landed fish. His head lolled back, mouth slackened. A swelling and purple mark were beginning to rise on his jaw and she grinned maliciously. Good. Then in sudden worry, she felt at his jaw, afraid that she might have broken it. She had kicked him pretty hard.

It wasn't, and she sighed in relief. Much as she didn't like the man—detested was the better word for it—she didn't want to become a murderer, and she'd been afraid that she might have blocked his windpipe. She looked from him and then to the bed, sighing. Then she bent down and started to heave him on to the bed. It was a long hard pull, for he was a pretty big man and she was on the slight side. She could still remember what her self-defence instructor had told her, when he had thrown her time and time again.

'You're smaller than I, Leslie! I can beat you every time. I have the strength. I have the power. I could break your neck with one blow to your jaw! Men are stronger, and they are usually faster. What you have to do is use the one thing that you have in abundance: your brain. Outsmart 'em, Les. And I'll help you work on how.'

She finally managed it, with a great deal of difficulty, and then she took his top sheet to tear it in wide strips, from top to bottom. She tied him up as tightly as she could, and as thoroughly. She didn't much care about his comfort. He wasn't going to get loose, and that was all there was to it.

After she had him firmly bound, she searched around the room thoroughly. There was a hand gun in the top drawer, and she took it. It was an automatic, so after some rummaging around she found a few extra clips in another drawer. She took those too. Then she yanked his pillow from under his head, threw it on the floor for a cushion, and settled herself down for a comfortable wait.

She was in for a long one.

She was starving by the time darkness had well and truly settled over the island. The sun had been dipping fast when she had entered the room with Paul, so objectively it was not that long before she deemed it safe to make a move. But together with nervousness, hunger, and exhaustion, the time seemed interminable. She could thank whatever god was watching over her that Paul had left instructions not to be disturbed until he emerged from the room. It gave her a bit of security for a time.

She stood, fingers trembling, and listened at the door closely for a long moment. Just before she was about to brave slipping out the door, a sound caught her attention. It was coming from the bed. She turned and whitened as she realised what she had forgotten.

She'd left the most obvious and dangerous thing

Look what we've got for you:

Get 4 FREE full-length Harlequin Presents® novels.

Plus
this handy compact manicure set

Plus
a surprise free gift

▼ PLUS LOTS MORE! MAIL THIS CARD TODAY ▼

Harlequin's Best-Ever "Get Acquainted" Offer

Yes, I'll try the Harlequin Reader Service under the terms outlined on the opposite page. Send me 4 free Harlequin Presents® novels, a free compact manicure set and a free mystery gift.

108 CIH CAMY

PLACE STICKER
FOR 6 FREE GIFTS
HERE

NAME _____

ADDRESS _____ APT. _____

CITY _____

STATE _____ ZIP CODE _____

PRINTED IN U.S.A.

Don't forget...

...Return this card today to receive your 4 free books, free compact manicure set and free mystery gift.

...You will receive books before they're available in stores and at a discount off retail prices.

...No obligation. Keep only the books you want, cancel anytime.

If offer card is missing, write to: Harlequin Reader Service,
901 Fuhrmann Blvd., P.O. Box 1867, Buffalo, NY 14269-1867

of all. She ran back and, shaking fiercely, stuffed a sock into the man's mouth, tying it in place with another sock. Just as she finished knotting it and put his head back down, he opened his eyes and glared at her silently. She put her hands to the sides of his cheeks and smiled down at him with her slow smile.

'It's all or nothing now,' she told him in perfectly fluent Spanish. His eyes widened in shock. 'You know it and I know it. I won't apologize for the kick to your jaw—you deserved it, and worse.' She backed away as she heard a soft, muffled groan. She was chuckling under her breath as she listened again at the door. He must have one hell of a headache by now. It gave her a sense of satisfaction to know that he would be reclining without his pillow.

The night was alive with creature sounds: the buzzing of winged things, a raucous cry from overhead, rustles in the undergrowth. Leslie slipped out of the barracks and sped on light winged feet to the dark shadows of the bushes by the building. There were two buildings between herself and the barrack—a deadly obstacle course. For the first time, as realisation dawned on her of the hopelessness of the situation, she felt the pangs of despair. The time was approaching midnight, and most of the lights were off, but there were a few still with gleaming yellow shining from windows. That meant a few were still up and about. And there were two guards at the barracks doors. And the hostages were dismally outnumbered, on an island, with men who were trained to kill. She sagged against the side of the building and muffled a sob. She was so very tired.

But then she pushed herself and straightened away from the wall. It was all or nothing. She went down into a cautious crouch, slipped forward out of the bushes, hissing at the rustle of leaves, and sprinted for the first of the two buildings. It was a nightmarish run. Her clothes were light and must show up like a blurred beacon, she thought nervously. The night air was cool, and she jerked violently to the side as something brushed her cheek—a mosquito. She then had to laugh soundlessly at her overreaction.

Then she had to steel herself and make the run again to the second building. The worst was ahead of her. Presumably everyone would be relaxed and off guard, but the two men stationed at the barrack doors would be alert. The building was further off from the others, which would mean, on the favourable side, less chance of anyone hearing strange sounds. On the negative side was that she had to somehow run without being seen from here to there, over open ground, and quietly overpower two armed guards. She quailed at the thought.

Her eyes narrowed on the dark silhouette of the building, which was her goal. The barrack doors opened to the right from where she was. It would have been disastrous if they'd been facing the other buildings. If she sneaked around to the left of this building, ran for the cover of the undergrowth some distance away, and came at the building from directly behind it, there was a chance she would not be seen. The guards, though alert, could not be expecting any trouble. Their charges were locked safely away in a building which they could not get out of without considerable noise and effort, due to the windows installed. There was no way out other than the doors they were charged to guard. And there was no reason for them to suspect their commander to be outsmarted and physically overcome by a mere slip of a woman.

Then again, there was still a good chance that someone would see her.

Leslie gritted her teeth and didn't give herself time to think about it anymore. She turned and ran for the forest. She was partially blocked from the guards at the barracks with the building that was still between herself and them. She reached the darkness of the forest's edge, breathing hard, waiting. As she listened and strove to get her breathing under control, she found her senses heightened, her hearing almost painfully acute, and her eyes dilating, for she could now see better in the dark. She was getting her night sight. Though the forest was cool, she drew her hand across her forehead and found herself drenched in nervous sweat. Then she started to edge along the undergrowth. It was a distance of about fifty metres. Then she looked from her position to the building across the open, naked ground. It looked like a mile of exposure, instead of only another fifty metres or so. Staring at it, she realised as she took in the position of the other buildings, that she

needed mostly silence now, instead of speed. The
risk of exposure would come from the guards
themselves. So instead of breaking and running for
it in that quiet night, she dropped down to her
stomach. Under her hands were a few rocks. She
shifted off them as they dug into the fleshy part of
her hands painfully and then fingered them
thoughtfully. A few made it to her shirt pocket.

Then she wriggled forward. Of all of the bad
experiences in that day, this, she found, had to be
the worst. The need for silence hampered her
movements to a certain extent, and so she had to
inch over that open ground, feeling horribly
exposed. She could just guess how her light
summer clothes showed up against the dark green
grass. She flinched away violently from every
imagined sound. It was terrible. Any moment she
expected to have her flesh searingly torn apart by
the staccato from machine gun fire.

Leslie stood up at the back of the building,
leaned against it, and panted, though she'd done
no more running as yet. Her composure was
slipping, she felt, and deliberately made herself
take deep, even breaths. It didn't calm the wild
pounding of her heart, but it did make her hands
steadier. She had a horrible suspicion that anyone
standing within five paces of her would be able to
hear her erratic pulse beat. She pressed her hands
against the building and then slowly drew the gun
out of her waist band. Never had this whole idea
seemed so wild and impossible; in that moment,
she knew she was most likely going to die within

the next several minutes. There were no windows at the back where she was, since in the inside there were the bathrooms, but if she could have, she would have peeked into the dark barrack to satisfy a craving to see her friends again.

Hopelessly she hefted the gun in her hand and edged around the building, on the far side, away from the other buildings and facing the forest. She had absolutely no idea of what she was going to do.

It was there that Leslie fell into a marvellous, once in a lifetime piece of luck. She slowly, slowly inched her way to the front of the building and stopped just around the corner from the two guards. There she stood, quaking and shaking, simply unable to force herself around the corner to that almost certain death. And as she hesitated just that one moment, she heard the guards murmuring together good naturedly. And at their words, she sagged against the building in profound relief before slipping back to the other end.

The two men had been quarrelling half heartedly in the lazy way workers will when they have to do something they personally consider unnecessary. Neither one wanted to take the half hour routine stroll around the building as there was nothing on the other side, anyway, and both were feeling relaxed. But one of them had to do it.

As Leslie tensed on the other side of the building, she realised with a jolt just how dangerous this really was, for she had no inkling of which side of the building the guard would come around. She

very nearly panicked, until she saw from her side
the lazy walking figure of the guard coming
round—the second piece of fabulous luck. She
waited until she heard the swish of his feet against
the grass, tensed until she felt her senses tingle with
the awareness of him just around the corner.

Only one chance—her foot, with all of the force
of her swinging body behind it, connected with the
man's midsection and he went down with only a
wheeze of air exhalation. Then she was dropping
down hard on his chest and pressing the gun
against his mouth as it opened. The man's eyes
bulged; he understood the silent message. She
edged the machine gun out of his nerveless fingers
and shoved it far enough away so that he couldn't
reach for it. Then she made him roll over to his
stomach, with his hands and arms high above him,
and she whispered in Spanish, 'Tell your friend
you have to make a trip to the forest.' Even in the
relative darkness she could see his eyes glitter as he
stared at her. She prodded with her gun and the
man promptly called out the message. She then hit
him over the head with the butt.

And realised her second colossal mistake of the
night. Her gun, filched from the commander's
room, had been on safety the entire time. If the
man had but known it, her threats had been totally
useless.

She shivered violently, as if with a sudden severe
chill as she realised that she probably couldn't
have shot the man anyway. She couldn't do
murder in cold blood.

She had no time to waste. She slipped from around the building and tiptoed to the front, and got one of the hugest, though harmless, shocks of her life. She happened to casually glance to the darkened windows of the barrack and nearly fell over as she saw the chest and shoulders of someone silently staring out, not two feet from her.

Scott. She glided to the window and her hand went involuntarily to the glass. His hand silently touched there, and though she felt only cold, hard smoothness, it was as though he had touched her with his warm hands. He urgently shook his head and motioned for her to run away. She shook her head in return. He was so very close, and large and vitally real, and yet so far away. There was nothing he could safely do to help her. She caressed the glass between them, saw his hand clench into a huge, impotent fist, and then slipped silently to the front.

She shrank against the side of the building and then dropped to her knees, rationalising that someone would not automatically look for eyes peering around a corner at knee level instead of shoulder level. It was an unnecessary precaution, for the guard was intent on something in front of him. It took her a second or two to realise that he was, in fact, merely rolling a cigarette and swearing at his clumsiness in thick Spanish. She took one of the rocks in her pocket and threw it over his head to the other side of him.

And made the third of her biggest mistakes in that night. Because of the darkness and the optical illusion from moonlit shadows, and her own inability to expose her arm around the corner, she merely managed to hit him in the head. She saw his head jerk up and he swore as he upended all of his loose tobacco all over his shirt. *Stupid!* she raged silently, and then he was coming around the corner of the building.

But Leslie's luck had not yet worn out. The guard came easily, machine gun casually slung over his shoulder, expecting to find nobody but his fellow guard, indulging in a little horseplay. There was no logical danger. All of the hostages were safely contained and accounted for. And Pedro was going to get it for making him spill the tobacco down his clean shirt.

Leslie, in the split second she had in which to think, came to an instant decision that was nothing short of brilliant. She stuck her gun in the back of her waist band, and when the guard came around, she half whispered, half called to him in a throaty Spanish, 'Sh, and come, *amigo*.' She lifted her arms high. Her accent was excellent, and she fervently hoped that he would think she was the young Spanish flight attendant, out for a bit of fun. 'Pedro already got his fun.'

The man came close as Leslie frantically wondered if the woman was even on the island, or if there were any women at all. But he had not yet had time to get suspicious, since all of the guards knew that none of the hostages spoke any Spanish. She sighed in relief, as there were apparently women on the island, and brought her knee up viciously to the man's groin. She hit dead on target and he doubled over in agony.

But her luck had run out. This man was made of sterner stuff than the first guard, and he brought his arm out in a chopping blow that caught her on the collarbone and nearly broke it. Her body slammed against the side of the building, and she knew a horrible sinking feeling. This was it; the advantage of surprise had been stretched too far this time; she'd lost the edge that she'd had over the men. She watched for him to bring up his gun and blow her away.

But she had forgotten the man's perspective of the scene. He had been at first pleasantly surprised and then painfully, and he was about to teach this mischievous, vicious little Spanish woman that the male was still the boss. His hand cracked across her cheekbone and she couldn't still the cry of pain at the blow, her head snapping sharply. Then she dropped to the ground and kicked as hard as she could at his knee cap.

She missed, and her foot grazed his knee, painful, but not crippling. Then his foot jerked out and he kicked her in the stomach, which made her double up on herself, wheezing as white sparks exploded in her abdomen. For all of her self defence lessons, this was the first time Leslie had ever been actually fighting for her life, and she was profoundly shocked at the pain in her own body. Even as her mind screamed for her to overcome the pain and strike back before it was too late, the man hit her again, and as this was aimed at her throat, she immediately started to choke and fight

for air. Could he have broken her neck? she
thought dazedly.

He was on top of her and his hands ripping her
blouse off, and there was a splintering sound.
Leslie couldn't believe her ears, because cloth
should rip, not splinter, but she couldn't dwell on
that for the gun was really digging into her back
now, and that hurt more than anything, though
the man was biting at her neck where he'd hit her,
and that was hurting quite a bit now, too. Then
suddenly his weight was off her.

Scott had moved soundlessly to the front of
the barrack, and when he heard a feminine cry
of pain, he had bolted for the window. He and
both Jarred and Wayne had kept a silent,
wakeful vigil, hopelessly watching, and the
incredible surge of pride and fear for her safety
had overwhelmed Scott when he realised that she
was creeping right by his window. But at strange
sounds now ensuing, he knew that something
was terribly wrong, and he snapped out lowly,
'Keep everyone quiet and the lights off,' as
people started to stir from sleep, aroused at the
upheaval. What he saw when he looked outside
made something inside of him snap. Leslie was
on the ground, fighting desperately while the
guard ripped her clothes off her. The build-up of
his rage and feeling of impotence boiled up, and
with a feeling of savage primitive joy he simply
hurled himself right through the window. It was
positioned at nearly shoulder level, so he had
quite a drop, but he went head first into a body

roll and came to his feet, a murderous two hundred pounds of raging male body hurtled right at the off balance guard.

As the man was lifted off her, Leslie felt a moment of simultaneous panic and relief. For better or worse, at least that animal was off her, and she could move, albeit painfully. Then the two men were grunting and plunging as they struggled, and Leslie felt an upsurge of hope. One of them stepped excruciatingly on her shin and she cowered away, feeling terribly bruised and helpless. She tried to distinguish between the two men and couldn't. One of them was taking a horrible beating, and she knew she should try to get up to help, but she couldn't get strength to her quivering limbs.

Then one man smashed his fist right into the other's face, and the other man went down as peacefully as a baby. All Leslie could do was gasp and shake, and the victorious one straightened and turned her way. He was a big, solid, bulky shadow and she shrank back from him. Then moonlight glinted on silver blond hair and she was jerked into Scott's arms.

He rocked and held her so tightly, it hurt her already abused body and she grunted in pain. But then his arms were loosening and his mouth dove down for a quick, intensive, soul shaking kiss, mouth open, teeth pushing, tongue penetrating. He reared his head up suddenly and whispered urgently, 'The other guard?'

She mumbled back, shakily, 'He's knocked out

around the corner.' She was still hurting badly and finding breathing painful.

He snorted shortly. 'You're incredible. Can you get the doors open while I tie these two up?'

'Sure,' she said, straightening wearily and fumbling at her top to tie the ends together in some semblance of decency. The utter exhaustion in her voice made his head snap up.

'Are you all right?' he asked her quietly, cupping her cheek. 'You didn't—the commander didn't do anything to you, did he?'

Even in the midst of her aching, trembling reaction, she could feel his tension and whispered back reassuringly, 'Nothing happened, other than he's going to have a sore head for quite some time. I got lucky.'

His head was turned away as he stared out to the forest, and then angled back at her sharply. 'You must have heard something very frightening, to take the chance that you did,' he commented quietly. His hand went to her back to help her to her feet. 'We'll talk in a few minutes—what the hell?' This was as his hand encountered the bulge of the gun in her waist band.

She drew it out and gave him the extra clips for good measure. 'From the commander's room. You keep it—it scares me half to death.' As he stood stock still with the implements in his hands, she glided to the front of the building, fumbled at the bolts, and slipped in.

The darkness of the interior was quite black in comparison to the moonlight illuminating the clearing. It also rustled, with people stirring and whispering furiously to one another, asking bewildered questions. The low voices stilled as she opened the doors, and then there was a concerted rush in her direction. Two large bulks nearly collided into her and someone grabbed her arms.

Wayne said, sliding his hand up to her hair, 'Leslie? Good God, are you all right?' In his low voiced question, as he hugged her convulsively, was a sharp relief.

Jarred said, with feeling, 'Dear Lord, it's the wonder lady.'

A nervous, middle aged feminine voice said sharply, 'If it's that slut back in here, I won't have her near me!' Several voices asked something that was all jumbled together as people talked at once, and Wayne hissed frantically for everyone to keep their voices down.

Of all the intensity of her frightening experiences, what Leslie found that she couldn't handle was the dark confusion, with too many voices babbling and low, fierce arguments being snapped out. She turned to Jarred, who had put his arm around her shoulders, and said quietly, 'I need my luggage. My blouse got torn.' He led her over to the wall where it had been stored. In the enveloping darkness she felt no compunction about slipping out of the one blouse and shrugging on another, sure that no one could effectively see her.

Something black blocked out the moonlight that was spilling in the open doorway, and Scott strode silently in to a chorus of guilty gasps and fearful exclamations. He said in a normal, though low voice, 'Calm down, everyone. It's just me, Scott Bennett.' He closed the door behind him and something metallic clanged to the floor. 'Don't turn any lights on, please. Leslie, where are you?'

'Here,' she replied briefly, tucking in her blouse. Someone banged against the end of a cot and swore vulgarly. Most, however, had quieted into a waiting curiosity.

Scott asked her concernedly, 'Are you sure you're all right?'

'I think so. A bit bruised, but otherwise intact.'

'What happened?' a man, sounding like the captain, asked sharply. There were murmurs at this, and one of the men muttered something that sounded rude.

Leslie replied lowly, her voice urgent, 'There are a few of us who know Spanish, but thought it best to hide the fact, on the chance that we might be able to overhear something. Today, I was standing near the commander while he was talking with one of the guards, and the gist of the conversation was that some of us were in great danger of being killed.' She listened to the stunned silence as everyone digested this information, and then several people spoke out sharply.

Someone moved, and a hand groped out of the dark to draw Leslie close to a long, powerful body as Scott hissed out, 'Keep your voices down!' The commotion ceased abruptly at the tone of authority. He tightened his arm on her shoulders as he then said, 'Go on, Les.'

So, as briefly as possible, she described the conversation, her own reaction and sudden decision, and the outcome of it. She admitted that she didn't understand much of what had been said, but that it was clear that six of them were in great peril, though she didn't know who aside from the four journalists.

As this was being absorbed, one woman said hysterically, 'So by coming back here and telling us, you've endangered us all!'

Leslie felt stunned. 'That is one perspective, I suppose,' she admitted, shaken. Could it have been her third colossal mistake of the day? She felt suddenly, absurdly close to tears and so utterly discouraged she could have lain down and died from it. Her whole body sagged against Scott's upright support, and his fingers tightened convulsively on her upper arm to keep her from falling, his other arm coming around to hold her close.

And she wasn't by herself anymore, facing terrible odds, as the woman received a blistering cut down from Wayne while Jarred said sharply, 'Madam, you are a fool if you think to believe from the casual conversation of hijackers and killers that you are in any way safer than the most imperilled of us!'

'We don't have time for this,' Scott said hardly. 'The main point right now is that we are alive and for the moment safe, and I fully intend to stay that way. Captain, is there enough fuel in the plane to get to Florida?'

'Yes.' The bald reply was a refreshing encouragement.

'How much time would you need to get us off the ground?'

'A few minutes, no more. Just long enough to turn the plane around and position it for taxiing down the strip. There's not much room to waste.'

'What about taking off in the dark?'

'Rather risky, since I'm not familiar with the clearing and the strip is so short.'

A moment of apparent thought, while Scott's hand rubbed absently up and down Leslie's back. She shivered. 'It can't be helped,' he said finally. A murmur arose at this. He said sternly, 'Quiet down, before you undo all of the good that Leslie did by risking her life! Jarred, Wayne, you two come with me to make sure the way to the plane is clear.'

As they both assented, the captain spoke again, voice sounding strangely disembodied in the dark. 'We'll need a way to board. Perhaps a crate or two, or that ladder, if you can find it.'

'Right.'

One of the men spoke up—who, Leslie couldn't tell, for she didn't know them all. 'Do you need help?'

Scott paused. 'I'd like help, but there are only three weapons, and any more than three would be a liability, not an asset. Thanks.' Another pause, and then, 'If we take any longer than forty minutes,' he said, 'I would run for the forest. If you hear anything unusual at all, run without looking back. If our secrecy is lost, then so is the plane. And above all, when we come back, be ready to leave, and don't take anything you can't run with.'

A murmur of voices, a soft, feminine protest, and exasperated male retort, and Leslie was pulled by that strong arm around her shoulders. She went forward on her toes, her hair was grasped and head tilted up, and then Scott was silently, fervently kissing her. Her mouth fell open and she unconsciously melted against him. A quake shook his sturdy frame, and he whispered merrily, 'Not now, Les, but maybe when I have more time.'

She gasped at the mirthful implication, and then reached out with both questing hands, for suddenly he and the other two were gone.

CHAPTER SIX

THERE was nothing but darkness, and the rustling, whispering movements of unseen living beings. Leslie found this strangely unsettling, and she backed until she had the wall behind her, then sank to the floor with a sigh. She groped to her right, and her hand encountered her luggage. She ticked off an automatic list in her mind: there was nothing of value, except the picture of Dennis and Jenny. She rummaged for it, and then gripped the frame in an agony of indecision. What should she do?

She berated herself with a brutal lack of restraint for having brought it in the first place. She knew better. She, of all people, knew that she had to be able to move at a moment's notice, and to be fully prepared to leave all belongings. Mobility was the key, and it was brought home forcibly to her now.

She had other pictures of the two, though not with the same memories as this one. Reluctantly she slipped it back into her luggage, and she resigned herself to never seeing it again. The choice, though painful, was obvious. The dead had to make way for the living.

People were whispering all around her, shuffling about, and someone was crying softly. Leslie had a brief mental image of the tense, strained features of the middle aged woman waiting for her husband, and she knew a surge of compassion. These people did not choose for this to happen to them. She became suddenly aware of the difference between herself and the other hostages.

Leslie's whole perspective took a shift. The difference. It was there, permeating her entire life. She was not any better than these people, not as good as some. God only knew, she struggled with her failings, with her petty feelings and occasional twinges of maliciousness. But there was a difference, a slight difference perhaps, and until now quite unconscious. The basic reality was that she was a creature of instinct, attuned to her animalistic nature. There was a beast living inside of each human animal, right alongside every intellectual brain, whispering in its sleep, nudging the human sometimes so gently, the brain's intellect did not even know that it was being manipulated. But Leslie caught a glimmer of understanding, as she realised how she had been thrust into the violent, brutal, physical fight for survival. She operated closer to her own instinctual awareness than most did. She was an animal, and always had been an animal. The difference was that she knew it now.

The implications of this soul searching conclusion were too colossal to explore right now. This cast a different light on her whole life, including that dismal mistake she had made with Scott. She would have to think about it. She was convinced that there did not have to be a conflict

between the mind and the body. She thought of
that overwhelming sexual need to be satisfied that
had gripped her, and felt a slow warmth suffuse
her whole aching body. Fear of entrapment,
aching, a strange yearning, shame—How could
there not be a conflict? She sighed and finally
managed to push it aside for good this time. She
had lived with opposing forces from within and
without all of her life. It would do no harm to
shelve it for a little while longer.

Providing they all survived, that is.

She eased away from the wall and sucked in her
breath at the stiffening soreness of her bruised
muscles. Then she made her way to the door. A
male voice asked sharply, 'Who's that? What are
you doing?'

It was the captain. She whispered, 'It's just
Leslie Tremaine. I was going to check on the two
guards. Do you know what time it is?'

'They've been gone twenty minutes.' She caught
a fleeting glimpse of his luminous digital watch
and it looked oddly bright. 'I'll come with you.'

She made no demur, and was indeed glad of the
company. Someone whispered a question, and the
captain answered, while Pat—Leslie would know
that voice anywhere by now—snapped with the
first sign of irritable tension she'd exhibited, 'This
waiting is going to kill me!'

'Please try to talk as little as possible,' the
captain requested softly. 'We'll slip back in about
five minutes.' With that they were out and around
the side of the building. The guards were trussed

up quite efficiently, and Leslie briefly admired Scott's neat knotting while the two no doubt thought murderous thoughts. 'I wanted to ask you,' the captin said very quietly, 'if you really were all right.' Her head tilted. 'I saw your struggle with the guard.'

'Well, I could be better, I suppose,' she murmured, 'but I'll certainly live. No, honestly, I'm battered but fine.'

'You appeared quite efficient at first.'

She chuckled softly. 'You are very delicate with your enquires. I took self-defence courses because my line of work can be hazardous, travelling through troubled countries like I do. But no, captain, I don't have any idea of what the commander meant by his remarks any more than you do.' I would have kept silent if I had, she thought. But the magic help she had hoped for had not appeared. Whoever was supposed to be working in some kind of undercover capacity was not in the group after all.

'Forgive my curiosity.' She heard his smile as she leaned tiredly against the side of the building. 'I couldn't help but wonder. You did overcome two adversaries larger than yourself. You are quite a woman.'

She sighed, looking out over the forest. 'Not really, sir. Desperation is a strong goad.' Queer, how the words echoed in her mind.

'Yes. It will be daylight soon.' The statement held heavy implications, and she flinched away from his unspoken question. She had asked it of

herself, as she was sure everyone had in the
darkened building.

She spoke with great conviction, though. 'Then
the sooner they get back, the better.'

The smile was quite gone from his voice. 'Just
so.'

When the men did finally come back, it was
anticlimactic. One moment Leslie was staring out
into the silver shadowed moonlit emptiness, and
the next moment a hand closed around her upper
arm gently. He was that quiet. She whirled with a
gasp, and then nearly laughed aloud, and then
nearly cried. In an instant she had herself under
control, but that lack of composure had her hand
clenched convulsively into the front of Scott's
shirt. She became aware of what she was doing
and let go, but her hand was captured and held
tightly. There were soft exclamations of relief.
Someone gripped her shoulder and squeezed, but
she couldn't see if it was Jarred or Wayne.

'Everything's ready,' Scott told the captain
lowly. 'We'd better get moving. We don't have
much time before dawn. We're going to take it in
three groups, ten each. The captain and the crew
are in the first set, along with the older members of
the group. Wayne will take you. Jarred will lead
the second group in ten minutes and I will guide
the third. Get your group together, Wayne, and
get out of here. And for God's sake, everyone keep
quiet, for the rest of us.'

A quick low head count sounded off. People
shuffled to the door. Leslie backed against the wall

again, feeling confused and disoriented, and upset by the jumble of unseen movement. The door was black as the group filtered out, and then silver moonlight shone in again.

Scott's voice came out of the darkness again, vital and controlled. She felt better just to listen to him. He said softly, 'All right, Jarred goes next. Get all the women together.' Shuffles, exclamations, soft feminine murmurs. 'Leslie? Where are you?'

She spoke up without moving. 'I think the married couples should go next, and the man with his wife back in the States. And Pat should go.'

A swift movement, and Scott was there, grabbing her shoulders so hard she grunted. 'Don't be stupidly noble,' he hissed intensely.

'I'll be what I damn well please,' she gritted.

'You're a fool.'

'It's my choice.'

Their argument was abruptly decided for them. One woman spoke up decisively. She would not go without her husband. This sentiment was echoed by other feminine voices, while a male asked querulously, 'Why do we have to go in separate groups, anyway? Why can't we all just leave now?'

'Thirty is too many, too noisy. We'd never make it to the plane with a group of thirty. Ten is quieter, quicker. In smaller groups we may just make it. In a large group we'd be heard in a minute. Get ten together, Jarred, and get out of here. Anyone with a husband, wife or children go with him. Move it!' A scuffle, and then a convergence of people at the door.

Jarred whispered, 'Hold hands, everyone. We don't want to lose anybody.' The large blackness glided out and away.

'Okay, who's left?' Scott asked wearily. Voices chimed in, and Leslie jerked at Pat's nuances wafting through the others.

'Why didn't you go with the other group?' she asked, moving over and grasping the younger girl's hand. She could almost see the grin that must have spread over Pat's gamine features.

'I didn't have a husband, wife or child,' she giggled, and Leslie impulsively hugged her.

Scott had moved to the open door and was staring out, a black silhouette, and tense. 'I don't like it,' he uttered tersely. 'Something's going on.' There was an appalled silence. Then everyone rushed to the door. 'We're not going to wait. Get ready. Don't lag behind. Run for the forest brush to the left. We're going to make a wide circle in the brush, and then run for the plane, which is about fifty yards from cover.'

After such decisive orders, he seemed strangely hesitant, and his head lifted to look over the group as if searching for something. But then Leslie thought that she had imagined it, for he was turning and gliding away without a sound. The others followed as quickly as they could. She tiredly wondered, when will this nightmare night end? From the time she had left the commander's bedroom to the present, about an hour and a half, had seemed to be forty forevers. She then became aware that she was still holding on to Pat's hand, and that the other girl was gripping her fingers just as desperately. Under cover of the bushes, Scott said tersely from somewhere close ahead of her, 'Be as quiet as you possibly can. When I shout out, break and make for the plane. Don't hesitate and don't look back, just run like hell.'

And then came a period of wriggling through the brush and twisting around fallen tree branches, never more than ten feet from the open clearing, sweating, fearful, tense. The group was filled with a sense of frantic urgency. Leslie and Pat stuck close together, drawing comfort from each other's presence. Leslie could hear the younger girl's heavy breathing as physical exertion taxed muscles unused to such exercise.

'Are we getting close?' Pat whispered, panting. Leslie considered and then shook her head unconsciously, forgetting about the dark.

'About halfway there. It's a big clearing. Sh.'

And there were far off shouts, lights being turned on, general commotion. Leslie risked a quick look over her shoulder, around the edge of a bush. 'My God, they're in the barrack!' she hissed out.

Scott heard her and he lifted his head. They were about a hundred and fifty yards from the plane now and approaching it fast. But now there were men running at the other side of the clearing, black against glaring, yellow, streaming light, and there was no more time for stealth. They would be

horribly exposed, but there was nothing else for it.
'Now!' he snapped, breaking cover. 'Run, get out
of here! Don't look back!'

The group bounded out like flushed rabbits.
Leslie bent her head and sprinted for the plane,
feeling the muscle in her sore shin cramp. The men
were shouting, running their way. But the group
had enough of a lead that they just might make it.
Then there was a thumping sound and a cry of
pain. Leslie jerked to a halt as if yanked back by
the end of a leash. She whirled. It had been Pat.
She raced back to the fallen girl and helped her to
her feet.

'My ankle!' the young girl gasped. 'I twisted it!'

Strength lent by desperation had Leslie yanking
Pat's arm across her shoulders and turning to
stumble back to the plane. They were behind the
others now. Pat was gritting her teeth in pain and
doing her best to hop along. Leslie panted and
knew they wouldn't make it in time. There were
sounds of shots being fired behind them. Scott was
racing back, skidding to his knee and sending a
spray of machine gun fire that scattered the
pursuing men. They limped to him and Leslie
coughed out, 'She's too heavy! Take her, quick!'

Scott gave her a look, wasted no time, and
swung the younger girl up with the machine gun
slung on to his shoulder, racing back to the plane
with no apparent lessening of his speed from the
load. Leslie raced on beside him, and everything
about her ached, from her stomach cramping
where she'd been kicked, to her throbbing

collarbone and the bruised muscle in her leg. Gun fire spurted behind him. Leslie faltered and Scott, attracted by the alteration in her stride, glanced back worriedly. But she was running smoothly again, with every appearance of ease.

'Just tripped!' she panted. 'Get her to the plane!' His fleeting fear allieviated, he raced on to the monstrous machine which was rumbling to instant life. He pulled ahead of Leslie.

Leslie had put everything into that brief moment of acting, when she had run several steps as though nothing was wrong. It had worked; he was nearly there now. The blow to her leg which had barely hurt at first rapidly consumed her mind in a swift burning pain. She fell to the ground, face a mask of despair. Her hands had convulsively gripped her right leg.

She brought one of her hands away, and it was dripping with blood.

CHAPTER SEVEN

LESLIE heard the guns behind her, and she put her head to the ground. There were shouts from the plane, and curses. The men behind her were approaching fast. It had all happened so incredibly swiftly. She knew the plane would take off: there were too many lives at stake aboard to risk all for just the one who didn't make it. She sobbed drily and turned her face to the cushiony turf.

And the plane's engines were whining as it ponderously turned right where it sat. Thirty seconds later, machine guns belting rounds into the metal hull, it plummeted down the clearing, out of sight in the darkness, and she felt a rush of air, the high, almost unbearable sound of take off. She tensed anxiously for any sounds of a crash.

The plane's whine smoothly died away.

She lay there dully, awaiting the inevitable discovery. Incredibly, she was nearly overlooked as men milled around the clearing, looking overhead and cursing furiously.

Someone stumbled over her. Hands yanked her up and she nearly fainted from the pain as she was jammed on to her feet, buckling over. A man shouted, 'One didn't make it! She's wounded!'

Orders were roared from some distance away,

and Leslie was slung on to the man's shoulder like a sack of potatoes. She was feeling quite odd by this time, drifting in a haze of blurred vision and burning fire. She wondered if the bullet was lodged in her leg or if it was just a flesh wound, with the bullet passing right through. There was a confusing passage, and some yellow light, and then they were indoors and the man was throwing her down to the floor with a malicious disregard for her evident discomfort. She lay where he had tossed her, in a crumpled heap. There was no reason to move. There was no escape.

She was thrown over on to her back with a well aimed kick, and she looked up into the wrathful, vengeful eyes of the commander. His face was discoloured on one side and swollen. She looked at his jaw with a dull satisfaction. All or nothing and she'd lost. 'What odd irony that it should be you to be left,' he said, chillingly, gloating. He squatted, and his face was too near. She shut her eyes wearily. She was slapped so hard her whole body rocked. Then it began. 'Who do you work for?'

'The CIA,' she mumbled, and was kicked.

'Don't try my patience with such sarcasm. Who do you work for?'

'The FBI,' she tried, and she wasn't kicked, so she considered the answer a success.

'When were you contacted?'

This she didn't know how to answer, and she thought a moment. 'Right away,' she ventured, and he appeared puzzled.

'And how much did Rodriquez tell you?' His

hand was clenched and ready, and she kept her eyes on it.

'Everything. We know all about your operation.' She was backhanded across her mouth and blood spurted. In a way she was grateful for being on the floor, because she was trembling so much she couldn't have supported herself in a chair if she'd had to. She felt the seepage of something wet down her trouser leg and didn't dare look. It trickled. The wound no longer hurt, as her whole leg was going numb.

'Liar!' he snarled, frustrated. 'He didn't know everything to tell!' He thought a moment, baffled and furious. 'This is much too easy. What are you up to?'

'It's simple,' she said, her words slurred now, her eyes glazing over. 'I haven't the faintest idea what you are talking about. I think you're quite mad, actually. I know I'm going to die sooner or later, and I'm telling you what I think you want to know, because I don't like being beaten.' And from sheer despair, she chuckled painfully, wryly, thinking what a strange ending to her life. She fainted.

The commander and the guard at the door stared at her in astonishment, totally thrown off by that queer laugh at the end. 'I hate to say this,' the guard ventured slowly, 'but I have the oddest feeling she's telling the truth.'

The commander sighed with impatience. She had fainted too soon. He would have her bandaged and then brought to. She was right. She was going to die. The commander was a vengeful man, and she had sadly trampled on his ego. He fingered the bruise at the side of his face and felt a grudging admiration, along with a renewed surge of rage. He would make sure she died unpleasantly for that.

'Of course she's telling the truth,' he said, and stalked out of the room.

A floating in yellow, brown and dull green haze. Her eyes focused on the man over her, who was bandaging her right leg with white strips of cloth that turned a spotted red as she watched. How long had she been unconscious? Perhaps fifteen minutes? There was no way of telling. She sighed wearily and it brought the man's head up. He was a stranger to her, older, with greying hair, and in his eyes was a sneaking compassion.

He said in Spanish, 'I am to tell the commander when you awake. He is out supervising the work. We are leaving the island within the hour.'

Her mouth felt lopsided, swollen, as she twisted one side. 'Am I to be killed before you leave, or after, at his convenience?'

The man looked away. 'I could delay going to him.'

It was quite an offer. If the commander ever suspected that this man had dared shelter her, he could be in danger. 'No need,' she whispered dully. 'The end is the same. I have to face it sometime.'

The man started to say something, but stopped as he looked into her eyes. They were on opposing sides. Though he felt sorry for her, he could not change his allegiance. He left the room.

After about ten minutes, during which she realised she was running a fever from her wound for the room would not stop moving on her, the man, who must be the doctor for the rebels, entered the room and behind him came the commander.

She turned her head away. The whole nightmare began again, with the relentless questions, the blows to her head and sometimes her stomach, his gloating, leering face. She just lay like a limp rag doll, and finally refused to answer his questions when she realised that he was determined to torture her no matter what she said.

He seemed to be infuriated, frustrated. She couldn't know that her passive response and lack of screaming and crying enraged the man more than anything. He was a man who lived by his particular code of power, which rarely failed to intimidate his underlings. And this slip of a woman, while he slapped her time and time again, was no more interested in him than if he had been a chair.

He stopped and stared at her. 'I will make you scream,' he said softly. 'I will take you for my pleasure and then give you to my men. There are three hundred out there. You will scream.'

'No doubt,' she whispered, eyes closed. She just wished it was over with. The doctor had given her something that made her feel very woozy. It helped. She wished her ear would quit ringing. He tended to slap her on one side, and it had passed beyond the merely painful to the excruciating as he abused bruised flesh.

He seemed to come to a decision and raised his fist again. She didn't even flinch. Maybe she would get lucky. Maybe one of the blows would kill her. But his head reared back and he cocked his head in a listening manner.

Leslie could hear far off commotion and wondered disinterestedly what was happening now. She tried to guess the commander's intention, and rather thought that he would kill her before bothering to transport her in an hour or so. Then she too cocked her head. The doctor's eyes widened. The faint sounds were shots. What could be happening?

She wasn't hearing as well as the others, for her ear was ringing annoyingly, and her whole body distracted her with throbbing agony. She felt like every bone had been broken and then trampled on for good measure. She could barely believe that it was early morning dawn, just two days after she had been leaving her apartment. Her leg was pounding, swollen against the bandages, and she saw that the white cloth was now quite red. She started to phase in and out of reality.

It was so strange. She could have sworn that she heard shouts and running feet down the outside corridor. The commander was backing against the far wall and pulling out his gun. But how could he have a gun? She had taken his. She shook her head, confused, and something slammed against the closed door with the force of a raging hurricane. The wood splintered, and a surging huge body careened into the room, ricocheting off the doorpost in a blur. The commander raised his gun and fired at the hurtling figure, but the other man was too fast. He lifted something large and black, and the commander's body slumped down the wall into a heap.

Now Leslie knew that she had passed into the queer realm of delirium, for the room's harsh light glittered off silver blond hair. And another man slammed into the room and pointed a gun at the doctor, who hadn't made a move. Jarred.

And Scott was dropping his ugly weapon and coming forward, his dark eyes wide and horrified, face rigid. Leslie's fever bright eyes regarded him solemnly. Her face was dark blue and purple along her right cheek, her mouth swollen on one side. Her slacks were torn off at the right leg above the knee, and the hasty bandage, unattended, was starting to drip vivid red blood. She looked like a fragile, battered child. He bent, mouth distorted, and gathered her oh, so gently into his arms and cradled her slim body against his chest. She bore absolutely no resemblance to the sunny, laughing, quick-witted creature he knew.

'D'you kill 'im?' she managed to say. Her mouth hurt so.

His answer was uncompromising. 'Yes.'

She sighed and it quivered through her whole body. His arms tightened fearfully, and he knew he should get her medical attention quickly.'S'nice dream,' she murmured, and her eyes closed. He knew by the sudden full weight of her head on his arm that she was unconscious.

Leslie looked up and smiled in lopsided surprise when she saw Scott enter the hospital room. He came forward and crinkled a smile down at her. 'Hello, how're you feeling?'

'Terrific,' she said, perfectly truthful. She grinned as he threw back his head and laughed at her. 'I'm serious. My leg is throbbing, my whole body is stiff and hurts if I even think of moving too fast, and my mouth is so sore I can barely chew my food. But I feel fantastic.' She looked around and chuckled. 'Have you ever seen so many flowers?'

Her eyes were on her, not the fragrant bouquets. 'Yes. Yesterday and the day before, but each time you were sleeping.'

She laughed in embarrassment. 'I didn't know. Well, your timing today is pretty lousy, too, I'm afraid. Wayne is going to be here any minute to pick me up. Three days is too long in a hospital, and I can't stand it any longer.'

Scott came forward and picked up her suitcase. 'I know. He's downstairs in the car, waiting at the pick up zone. I'm to bring you down.' Just then a young pretty nurse came in and smiled at Leslie and Scott. She was wheeling in a chair.

'Are you ready, Ms Tremaine?' Leslie nodded fervently, which made Scott laugh again, and the nurse grinned sympathetically. The nurse moved forward, but was stopped by Scott.

'I'll do that for you,' he said lazily, coming up on the other side of Leslie's seated figure. He picked her up as easily as if she'd been a child, and settled her into the wheel chair with an astonishing gentleness. Leslie pulled back her arm, which she'd placed around his neck. For a moment he was very, very close, and he stared into her eyes. His own held a strange, glowing expression, and she looked away in confusion. She heard his soft laugh. She leaned both elbows on the sides of the chair and covered her mouth with both hands, feeling oddly shaken.

The brief ride in the wheel chair was pleasant: to the elevator, and down to the ground floor, then outside to the waiting car. Her eyes widened as the nurse pushed her to where Scott directed, a strange car, and empty. 'Where's Wayne?' she asked him surprised. This wasn't his car.

Scott looked around curiously. 'I don't know. He must be waiting in the front lobby, thinking we were coming by that way. I'll go and get him after you're settled.'

'This isn't his car,' she said slowly, as he lifted her up and put her into the front seat as carefully as if she had been fragile china. Her suitcase, the stuffed animal Wayne had brought her, and the box of candy from Jarred, along with the walking cane she was to use until her leg headed completely went into the back seat. The bullet had been lodged in her upper shin and she had needed an operation to remove it, but the wound had been a muscle tear only. She would heal as good as new.

'It's my car,' Scott told her in explanation. 'We though it would be the best. It's bigger and more comfortable. It has better shocks than Wayne's does.' She nodded with a rueful grin. He was most probably right. Nearly anything was better than Wayne's car. Scott hesitated and asked her, as the nurse wheeled the empty chair away, 'Did you want your flowers brought down, too?'

She shook her head. 'No, I gave them to the nursing staff. They were beautiful, but rather overwhelming. Every single person from the hijacking sent me some! Wasn't that nice?'

Something passed over his face and was gone. 'Yes, very.' He walked around to the other side of the car and got in casually. Leslie looked at him in surprise.

'But aren't you going to get Wayne?' she asked him warily.

There was a strange smile hovering around Scott's well moulded lips. She wasn't sure she liked it. 'I lied,' he said cheerfully. 'Wayne didn't come along. I told him I'd pick you up.'

She cocked an eyebrow as she stared out the window at the Chicago traffic. He pulled on to a main street. 'I might have known you were up to mischief,' she said calmly. She leaned her head back against the rest and watched dreamily as the traffic swirled by. The last several days had been disorienting and confusing. She had been in a fever and couldn't really remember what had happened after her brusing confrontation with the 'commander', only four days ago. She had apparently been delirious, actually thinking that Scott and Jarred were there, along with the FBI force that had raided the island after the plane with the hostages had taken off. After that she couldn't even piece enough of her consciousness together to get her from there to here, which was to say, Chicago. She could only rely on what others had told her: that she'd been given immediate medical care and then flown to Chicago and admitted there. She had awakened in Chicago after the whole business, half inclined to think of it all as a dream, except for her painful leg and the ugly bruises on her body. They were real enough, though the bruises were now an ugly, yellowish black. Her hand went to her cheek automatically as she thought of this.

They were approaching the turn off that they should take to get to her neighbourhood, and Leslie briefly wondered if Scott even knew where she lived. That made her hope that Wayne had watered her plants for her. He probably had given the fern too much, and it would have root rot setting in. It was a struggle keeping her plants when her neighbour went on holiday and couldn't take care of them, her usual arrangement.

Scott stepped on the accelerator and flew by the turn off. Leslie turned her head sharply, felt the twinge in sore neck muscles. She cleared her throat as she tried to read his expression. 'You missed the turn,' she pointed out patiently.

'I know,' he said sweetly, and increased his speed.

Her brows shot up. 'You do? Then might I ask you just what the hell is going on?'

'I'm kidnapping you,' he told her conversationally, and crossed over to the other lane.

'You're what?' It was a scream of amazement. She deliberately relaxed rigid, hurting muscles and forced herself to take several calming breaths. She said more reasonably, 'What did you just say?'

'I said I'm kidnapping you,' he repeated, in a patient tone. Leslie felt her eyes widen in incredulity, then narrow in anger. 'You have,' he continued, 'a month's sick leave. I also have taken some time off. We are going to have a vacation together, and you are going to rest. The weather forecast is good. Do you like the country?'

'You're loony,' she stated with flat certainty.

'That is a distinct possiblility.'

'Turn around this instant and take me back. I won't stand for this,' she ordered, still inclined to think he was joking.

'No.' His answer was devastatingly simple.

She took a deep, unsteady breath and sighed, more upset than she'd at first thought. 'Why are you doing this?' she whispered. 'This is totally crazy, you know that.'

'I know that you have every reason to believe that.' He didn't look at her once.

'Are you going to explain yourself?' she asked, in a voice that trembled. He shot her a swift look, face gentling.

'Not yet. The seat tilts back, if you'd like to rest. You're not as strong as you would like to think.'

The utter truth of his words shuddered through her. She thought ironically that he would be surprised if he only knew how accurate his statement had been. She groped under the seat and pressed a control. The back slipped down, and she settled into a comfortable position. In a world that had bucked in an upheaval so tremendous it had nearly taken her life, her awareness had just been jolted, and she needed time to recover. Scott's actions were bizarre by most standards, and yet he had never seemed more calm or reasonable. Her eyes narrowed on him interestedly. He seemed— grimly purposeful, instead of raving mad. She wondered what his motive was, and spent some time trying to assess his actions. She couldn't come up with anything that made any sense. Shock rippled through her briefly as she realised how little she really knew about him. The swift car ate up the miles, the motion soothing. He was a good driver. She watched him, seeing the long silver blond hair, his stubborn jaw, the line of power stamped on his face. His hands were large on the steering wheel. She got a sudden vivid image of him wielding a deadly maching gun, and shook confusedly. The delirium had been so real. And she suddenly, softly laughed, surprising herself and him.

His eyes shifted to her and rested for a quick, assessing moment, blond brow cocked. 'That was an odd reaction. Not something I had expected, at any rate,' he commented, turning his attention back to the road.

She chuckled again as the humour of the situation hit her. 'Hijacked and then kidnapped within one week,' she burbled. 'It's unbelievable. If my family only knew!'

A strange look from him that she couldn't interpret, and then, 'Did any of your family contact you in the hospital?'

'Oh, yes. I was on the receiving end of a thirty minute lecture over the 'phone, interspersed with hysteria and guilt-inspiring tears,' she said wryly. 'It was all, naturally, as I'd always suspected, my fault. They all hope that by now I have learned a little sense, though they have realised they shouldn't expect it.'

And she wondered at the suddenly ferocious frown that lowered on his face for a good ten minutes. 'Naturally,' he said drily.

She watched his brooding countenance for some time as silence fell over them both. He asked suddenly, surprising her as he threw a glance her way, 'Are you afraid of me, Les?'

She was immensely taken aback at that, and frowned at his profile, at his odd question. 'No,' she replied slowly. She noticed how tensely she had been holding herself and knew that he had felt it. 'No.' She wondered many things, as her body then relaxed and exhaustion set in. She slept.

Evening set in and when Leslie opened her eyes the sun was setting to their left. That meant they were travelling north. She looked out and her gaze encountered heavily wooded land, which was only as she had expected. She adjusted her seat and came upright.

'How much further?' she asked, passing a weary hand over her eyes to dash away the blurred vision. She blinked.

His gaze swept over her. 'Almost there now,' he replied shortly. She nodded dully. His glance changed to a look of concern, but she didn't see it, as she turned to look out the window. She let her head fall back, feeling absurdly weak.

The drive continued for some minutes on that particular road, and then he made a quick turn to the left, drove some distance, and turned right. This road was considerably smaller, and not well paved. He slowed the car and eased on to a gravel lane. Trees were thick on either side, and the long reaching branches created a leafy canopy overhead, dark green, light green, brown and speckles of yellow sunlight. Leslie guessed that the wood covered some distance, for it was mature, with old oaks jutting towards the sky with majestic heaviness, and fully developed maples and beeches. She sat passively and let the quiet of the forest seep into her bones. This was a good place.

They soon came upon a small cabin that nestled into a small pocket made by several tall trees. Scott slowed, and then he pulled the car to a stop, parking at the side of the building. The engine stilled. He sat there for a few minutes, silently, head resting back, eyes taking in the scene. He seemed to be waiting. Leslie looked around her without comment. Then she reached back and took her walking cane, and opened her car door. Standing was rather painful, and she couldn't conceal her hiss as she put her wieght on her bad leg and felt the torn muscles and stitches take the strain. She leaned heavily on the cane.

Scott's quiet voice came from just behind her. She turned her head, not having heard him get out of the car. 'Are you all right?'

She nearly answered an automatic affirmative, and then wondered why she should bother to lie when it was so obvious. 'I don't know,' she replied shortly. 'I'll just have to take it one step at a time.' She then tried a few, using the cane awkwardly, her face a white mask.

'Don't overdo it,' he advised, watching her with a frown. 'The doctor said that you were to rest as much as possible. Give the leg time to heal before you use it.'

'After all, I'm not going anywhere, am I?' she said, with a bitter half laugh. 'You had this well planned, didn't you?'

Her question echoed rhetorically as he turned away, not bothering to reply. Instead, he mounted the steps on the porch and unlocked the front door of the cabin. Tired, depressed, in pain, Leslie just stared at the five porch steps and then grimly started forward. She felt foolish as she had to take each step with her left leg and pull her right up after. She didn't dare put that much strain on the wound. It was hurting badly enough as it was. On the third step she was gritting her teeth and

leaning more on the cane than anything else. She
heard an exclamation and Scott came forward to
gently swing her up into his arms.

'I was only checking to see if the cabin was
cleaned, like I'd ordered,' he scolded. 'I would
have come back to help you if you'd waited.'

She lost hold of the cane and it clattered down
the steps to rest on the ground as he carried her
into the small cabin. Something greater than
weariness impelled her to let her head sink to his
broad shoulder. He could take the weight.

The front room was a comfortable living-room,
and he deposited her on the couch, which sank
down, invitingly soft. She looked around her with
interest. To her right was the front of the cabin,
and a large waist high picture window that looked
on to the porch. To her left was a counter with a
tiny kitchen behind it. Dead ahead were two
doors, and judging by the dimensions, she guessed
that whatever was behind the two doors was about
it as far as the floor plan went. There wouldn't be
room for anything else.

'Will you be all right while I bring things in?'
Scott stood, looking down at her. She nodded and
he disappeared.

He had to make several trips. First came her
suitcase, cane and things from the hospital,
which had been in the back seat. Then came
another suitcase of hers, along with his luggage
from the trunk, and she glowered at it. Wayne
had a lot to answer for when she got back to
Chicago. She'd trusted him with that apartment

key. Scott then brought in several paper bags and spent some time in the small kitchen, putting supplies away.

Frustration welled up in her, and then abruptly faded away. She was too exhausted to deal with the emotion. The day had taken more out of her than she cared to admit. Despite her throbbing leg, she stood and carefully limped over to the first of the two doors, using the doorpost as a support while she looked inside. A small bedroom with a single bed and dresser, a closet door and a door that led to a bathroom was all it held. She limped to the other door and peered in briefly. It was almost exactly identical, in reverse, to the other room. The bathroom connected the two rooms. The bed appeared to be made, but that could have been just a spread covering a naked mattress. She edged painfully forward, lifted a corner of blanket and stared at the neatly tucked in sheets. She crept on to the bed with a sighing of bed springs, and trembled as she stretched out. Her whole body ached. She turned her face to the wall and closed her eyes.

Some time passed while she drifted, and her leg insistently, exhaustingly, painfully throbbed. She slept fitfully as images chased through her mind. She tensed and started to sweat. The dark and the glaring light in her eyes, the guns and the cruel hands slapping her——

She jerked and cried out in fear as a hand descended to her shoulder. Then her eyes flew open and she stared at Scott, who towered above her, eyes compassionate. 'It was bad?'

She swallowed. 'It was bad.' His hand caressed her shoulder and then cupped her neck, falling away when he felt her tensing protest.

'What do you want from me?' she whispered.

He smiled at her easily. 'To eat supper. It's ready. Are you feeling hungry?' She was and nodded, and he picked her up to carry her into the kitchen. There was a small table with two chairs pushed against the other side of the counter, and he put her in one while she experienced the intense frustration of an invalid who wishes to do more than the body will permit.

The meal was already served and waiting, and she started to eat cautiously, then with great enthusiasm as she found the pork chops deliciously seasoned. A salad, and fluffy mashed potatoes completed the meal, with iced tea and coffee later on to drink. 'This is wonderful,' she said with her mouth full.

She was treated with a particularly captivating grin. 'I know,' he said impudently, and laughed at her speaking look. 'I will not be falsely modest. I freely admit that I like my own cooking.'

She smiled dutifully and then asked him quietly, 'What do you want from me?'

He merely smiled back and said nothing, as he swallowed the last of his supper and then stood to pick up the plates. She automatically started to help stack the dishes, but he forestalled her. 'Stop it,' he ordered. 'I do the work around here, and don't you forget it.'

She had to stare and then laugh, in spite of herself. It was such a funny thing to say. 'I'm not arguing,' she told him, holding up both hands in compliance.

She watched him wash the dishes, body moving with an economy of effort that was soothing to contemplate. But then she found her eyes travelling down his length, noting the snug fitting jeans against his buttocks and thighs, the shoulders occasionally straining against his plain shirt as he stretched to put away the dried utensils. She saw the long blond hair lying against his collar, and she wanted to run her fingers through the silky mass. She jerked her eyes to the coffee mug in front of her and concentrated on drinking it, movements jerky. Silence from Scott's direction. She looked up.

'You okay?' He was watching her closely.

She nodded, eyes falling away. When she looked up again, he was back at work, putting away the drainer and hanging the cloth towel up to dry. He turned and asked her, 'Would you like to move to the couch for a while?'

'No, I—I think I'll just finish my coffee here, and sit.'

'All right. Call me if you need or want anything.' He left the room. If she stretched her neck and looked over the counter, she could see him taking the luggage to the rooms and clearing the living-room. He put her chocolate on the table in front of the couch and disappeared for some time, first in one bedroom and then another. She could hear faint noises from each, and she tried to divine his actions. She pondered. The thing of it was, she had started to trust his judgement as she had come to know him better on the island. People reacted differently to stress, and a lot of the character could be inadvertantly revealed when one was under pressure. She had admired his quick reactions and calm strength. To be in the profession he was—and good at it, too—he had to have that core of stability.

She proceeded to the next step of her analysis. Her judgement had been sound. He had some objective, and it had to do with her. Seduction? She was not exactly what one could call devastatingly alluring with the multicoloured bruises abounding on her tired body. An involuntary grin quirked her lips. That surely could not be it, then. She had just reached the point where she was wondering if he was doing all this out of purely friendly motives, actually wanting her to have a nice, peaceful rest away from the pressures of civilization and city noises, when he entered the kitchen again.

He leaned against the counter and smiled down at her so warmly that she found herself responding back. His eyes were crinkled at the corners, white teeth against dark face. 'Have you come up with any conclusions yet?' he asked.

She felt surprised and then impatient with herself. Of course he would see that she was puzzled at all this. She got the nasty feeling that she was being manipulated, and she didn't like it. 'No,' she replied shortly.

'Keep trying,' he advised her, and then sighed, oddly weary. 'If you don't mind, I believe I'll go to bed now. The evening has slipped away rather unexpectedly. Do you want help to your bedroom?'

'No, thank you. You go on. I want to think some more, and it's not really that far. I can hop.'

'Don't be ashamed to admit that you're in pain, Les. I am within earshot, you know, and willing to help. I have a light touch and would be glad to give you a back and leg rub, if you'd like?'

She smiled reluctantly. 'It sounds good, but not tonight, thanks. Maybe later.'

'You have pain medication?' She nodded. He came forward and squatted in front of her, took her hands, and pressed a quick kiss into each palm. Then his head tilted up and he stared deeply into her eyes before smiling one last time. She got the strangest feeling that he was trying to convey some sort of wordless assurance and comfort. She was completely bewildered. 'I'll see you tomorrow, then.'

'Good night,' she whispered, as he left. She sat there for some time, and her mind went around and around in circles and in endless conjecture as she tried to fathom out this strange man she was with. She came up with exactly nothing, and finally, wearily, made her way to the empty dark bedroom that was hers. She switched on the light and looked around, smiling in gratitude as she took in the turned down covers, the laid out nightgown, the stuffed animal sitting on the pillow. He had even unpacked for her. Then her eyes went to the dresser and something bolted electrically through her chest. She nearly fell over from it, as her eyes stared and her heart pounded, and her breath left her lungs in an involuntary gasp of surprise.

There, sitting in solitary splendour, propped in a prominent position, was her framed photograph of Dennis and Jenny, laughing in the sun.

CHAPTER EIGHT

THE next morning, after waking, Leslie propped herself against the headboard and stared at the photograph of Dennis and Jenny thoughtfully. She smiled reminiscently at Jenny's cherubic countenance, the little girl's bright hair, her merry eyes. Her own filled suddenly.

'She is a beautiful child,' Scott said from the doorway. His eyes were on her, not the picture, compassionately.

Leslie bit her lip, feeling the ache in her chest, scrubbing at her cheeks hastily. He had caught her in a vulnerable moment. Her mouth trembled. 'You would have liked her,' she whispered, looking back at Jenny. 'She was so beautiful, so good natured and loving. She loved people. She would go to anybody and just give them that sweet smile of hers, holding her arms out for a hug.'

'She sounds like a special person.' That quiet voice came again, gentle, unobtrusive.

'Oh, she was. She was that rare child who can hardly ever be spoiled. She never threw temper tantrums. Do you know, the one thing I'd always expected, the one thing I took for granted, was that she would always be there.' A great wet drop splashed down her cheek, and she never noticed. Scott's eyes were filled with a huge sympathetic sadness. 'I always thought that I would get to watch her grow up, that surely she would outlive me, her mother. I'd counted on that.' Another tear shed; for Jenny, there would always be tears. 'Now all I have is cold glass and a dead impression. I'll never hold her warm little body again, never. The ache never goes away.' She put her empty arms around her middle. 'Please, just go away.'

Footsteps. Weight sinking to the bed. Scott leaning over, blocking her view of the photograph, vital, thrusting his presence on to her awareness. 'I can't do that,' he said lowly, gathering her up slowly and carefully. 'Your daughter is dead, but I am not. She can't hold you anymore, Leslie, but I can. Put your arms around me.' She didn't move. 'Do it. I'm alive and I'm warm, and I'm here. Hold on to me.'

First one arm crept up around his neck, and then another. Her face went down to his shoulder. Both his arms were full around her. His face went to her hair, hid there for a while, and then emerged and he started to kiss her. The kisses were gentle, soothing, giving, a soft rain down on the curve of her cheek, the arch of her neck, her forehead. When her face at last emerged, she was composed, though sad. 'The pain is an old one,' she told him. 'I'm sorry, I am not usually so grief stricken, but occasionally it does get to me.'

'I understand.'

'Do you?' she asked. She smiled wearily as he remained passively silent. 'Yes, I somehow think you do. Do you have any children? I know so little about you.'

He grinned faintly. 'To the best of my knowlege, no.' At that she had to laugh, shakily. 'Did you have anyone to share your grief with, Leslie— when they died?'

'I don't remember,' she said ruefully. 'I was pretty numb for a while. I don't think I did much talking about it. I'm not in the habit, you see.'

He sent her a look. 'I had noticed something of the sort.' She watched him as he seemed to hesitate, and then, 'I am not an effusive man. But, Leslie, I want you to know something. It's a small thing, nothing earth shattering, nothing I will ever impose upon you. I would say this one thing, and say it only once. The rest is up to you. I care. You can be alone if you would like, but you aren't alone now. If you want to talk, I will always listen. If you don't, then listen to the silence. This is a nice place for silence. I don't offer my friendship and allegiance lightly, but if you would have it, it is yours.'

Quiet. She felt as if she had been offered a precious gift. She was utterly still as she listened to the profound implications of his words. Scott was the kind of man that lifetime loyalties were made with. For the first time, she put her arms around him and simply hugged him tight. And he sat still as the implications of that washed over him. Then she pulled back and stared deeply into his eyes. 'Thank you, my friend.'

The words trembled between them before

melting into memory. Nothing more was said on it, but they both knew. A pact had been sealed.

'I've had my breakfast,' he said presently. 'Ham and eggs. Do you want some?'

'It's sounds terrific. I'll get dressed.' She hopped to the bathroom and quickly donned her clothes after washing, and then brushed her hair out. Then she took her cane and slowly limped into the other room. Scott was working in the kitchen, cheerfully whistling. With a sigh, she eased down into a kitchen chair, feeling as if she had trekked a mile. The cabin was sparsely furnished, but nice. Did he own the place, or rent? She knew so little about him. Her eyes went to the counter and she stared in surprise.

There sat the ring of car keys, quite out in the open. She leaned forward and picked them up, cradling the cool metal against slim fingers as she wondered. She turned and stared, eyes narrowed, at the back of the man fixing her breakfast. He was fully aware that she was there and watching. He must have heard her pick up the keys, for they had jingled musically. By his very deliberate movements, she knew that he was quite fully aware. He didn't turn to look at her. She jingled the keys louder, as she slouched comfortably in her chair and propped her sore leg forward. Scott looked briefly over his shoulder, and then turned to crack two eggs into the heating pan.

'This is a message,' she said calmly. 'What does it mean?'

He didn't bother to look around again. 'You know.'

'Yes, I do, but I want you to tell me.'

'It means that you are free to go whenever you like.' The eggs hissed. The fragrant smell of ham frying wafted to her nostrils, making them quiver. She sniffed the air appreciatively.

'And was that a recent development, or a planned manoeuvre?'

'I had never planned on keeping you here a prisoner.'

'Your methods on getting me here were rather unorthodox.' Leslie was beginning to be entertained, whereas yesterday she had been shaky, thrown off balance, and feeling unwell.

He chuckled softly. 'You're the type of person that always needs a little excitement in your life. What would you tell your family, otherwise?'

She threw back her head and laughed at that sally. 'You know,' she said, 'you've been manipulating me for a day and a half now. I must say, you've gauged my reactions well! I even know I'm being manipulated now, and do you know what? I don't care. I know that you've guessed what my reaction to this must be, and you are right, and I really don't care. You knew that I wouldn't be so callow minded as to pick up and scatter, not now. You waited until I had swallowed the bait, the serenity of this place and the curiosity, as I'm wondering just what you intend to prove or gain by all this. It's all gone just as you'd intended, right down the line.' She tossed the keys and they plinked on to the counter, skidding for several inches and stopping, splayed in solitary display. She did not look at the keys once after that. 'At least,' she concluded, with a strange half smile, 'so far it has.'

Scott turned around with the steaming, delicious smelling plate of ham and eggs and set it in front of her, with coffee, utensils, and the salt and pepper. Then he poured himself a cup of coffee and eased into the seat across from her. He was smiling. For a brief instant, she thought she saw deep relief in his eyes, but the impression passed by with a blink, and she couldn't be sure.

She asked again, and by now it was an automatic question, not one she really expected him to answer, 'What do you want from me?'

'If you have to ask, you aren't ready for the answer,' he replied simply. She stared at him while she reflectively chewed a bite of ham. He bore her scrutiny patiently, as if it was only what he'd expected, which, she was sure, was exactly the case.

She wondered how he would react to a little manipulation, himself.

That evening, after a peaceful, uneventful day spent reading—Scott having thoughtfully provided a box full of paperbacks of all kinds—Leslie stretched contentedly and sighed. She was favoured with a humorous glance, complete with whimsically raised eyebrow, as Scott's attention was diverted from his own story. 'I'm hungry,' she murmured and laughed. He was grinning, too. 'I know, I know. A big breakfast, super lunch, and I haven't done a blessed thing all day except sit, and I want to eat again? Well, it's true. I'm famished, and it's my turn to fix supper.' She started to struggle to her feet and was pushed gently back into the couch's soft depths as Scott stood and prevented her from rising. Her dark blue eyes danced up at him, unsurprised.

'I'll get it,' he said easily. 'Kick your feet up and relax, will you?'

'You're spoiling me,' she warned him, and he smiled down at her so nicely that her heart contracted queerly.

'But, of course I am,' he said cheerfully, and went to fix the meal.

She frowned heavily at the opposite wall, punched a cushion into shape, and subsided on to it thoughtfully. Yes, that was another definite, unspoken message from him. All deliberate, quite nicely executed, with that unknown goal in mind. She had to grin. It was all quite pleasurable too. She had never been treated so well, not even when she had given birth to Jenny. Sure, she had been taken care of, but there was a qualitative difference between the two. Scott's care was gentle, considerate, enjoyable and quite undemanding. Her grin became twisted as she remembered her mother's visit that month after having Jenny. Leslie had been made to understand, that whole, eternal month long, just how much her mother was giving her. By the end of the proposed thirty day visit, Leslie had nearly been climbing the wall in screaming frustration. Dennis had loved having her mother over. She had doted on him, that was for sure.

But then, in those days, who hadn't? He had been the man who could do no wrong, in the eyes of her family and the town. She shook her head at the thought, and then laughed ruefully.

'I like your laugh,' Scott told her as he came into the living room. She wrinkled her nose up at him. He was so easy to be with. No 'what are you thinking?', but just 'I like your laugh'. It occurred to her that not asking questions was another deliberate move from him.

'Thank you, kind sir. Scott,' she asked curiously, 'have you ever been married?'

He leaned against the side of the armchair. 'We're having a casserole,' he told her. 'It should be ready in about a half an hour. Do you think you can wait?'

'Oh, sure,' she replied absently. 'Why won't you answer me?'

He just looked at her. 'Is there a good reason why I should?'

'Well—I guess not. I was just wondering why you wouldn't want to. Do you have something to hide?' The stirring of curiosity was fanned by his uncommunicative replies.

'No, I've nothing to hide,' he replied, studying his nails with a slight frown. She let her eyes run over hard cheekbones, crooked nose, well moulded mouth. His gaze shifted to hers, shuttering lids and then a bright glittering glance that gave her a slight jolt. 'Any more questions?' she was asked softly.

The pang of loneliness that hit her took her totally by surprise. 'Would you even bother answering them?' she returned back, oddly bitter.

His eyes caressed her, and she caught her breath at the look, feeling a suffusion of warmth. 'No,' he said gently.

'Another clue,' she whispered musingly, wondering why she felt shaken.

'Think what you like.'

Supper was eaten in silence. Leslie retreated, and while she knew that he was watching her and gauging her reaction, she couldn't help it. She felt furious at her lack of control. What was he wanting? He was being everything that is attentive and thoughtful while leaving her room to breathe, and the situation should have been great. Then the question hit her and it left her with widened eyes, and a curiously frightened look. What was it that she was wanting?

She didn't sit in the kitchen this time while he cleaned up, but moved to the living-room to throw herself on to the couch, wincing at the warning twinge from her wound. Then she plunked her head into her arms and sighed gustily. She felt her mind whirling with uncertainties and questions.

After a while, she started violently as she felt two large, warm hands descend on to her shoulders. She tensed and would have pushed herself up, but he pushed her back down, murmuring, 'Stay right there, and I'll give you that back rub I promised you.'

She stayed where she was, rigid and immobile,

half inclined to get up and reject his overtures, but his touch was too relaxing, too gentle and rhythmic, much too enticing. She closed her eyes. Gradually, muscle by muscle, she relaxed and lay there passively while he worked on her shoulder muscles. She loved to have her back rubbed.

His thumbs dug into the pliant muscles between her shoulders while his long fingers gently rotated at the base of her neck. Then he stroked the top line of her shoulders to her upper arms, hypnotically systematic, over and over. He dug in deeply on either side of her spinal column, working all the way down to the small of her back. With the heels of his hands touching each other at her waist, fingers splayed out and curved around her sides, he wiggled his fingers underneath her weight. 'You're so slim, I wonder if I could span your waist with my hands,' he said amusedly. Her frustration and bafflement at his behaviour had dissipated, and she was feeling the warmth from his uncomplicated friendliness.

She lifted her hips up slightly and said, 'Try it and find out.' His hands shifted around, the tips of thumbs meeting at the base of her back, the fingers stretching around. She hissed at old bruises. 'Not too tight,' she grunted, remembering. 'I have a sore stomach.' He immediately slid his hands out from under her and continued with his rubbing.

'You do? Was it something I cooked?' he asked her drily, and she chuckled shortly.

'Hardly that. No, I was kicked in the stomach several times, and it's still tender.' She gave a surprised whuff! of pain as his hands convulsively tightened, as if in uncontrolled rage, and he then let her go suddenly.

'Sorry. I didn't know,' he muttered. 'I knew you'd been hit, but I didn't know the full extent of it. If only——' He bit off what he was going to say, telling her instead, 'I'll be more careful.'

But Leslie wasn't paying that much attention to him, as she started to do some deep thinking. She did say lightly, 'The man's got magic hands.'

He laughed lowly, and went back to work. Leslie jerked when he reached down and gently eased up her right pant leg. 'Relax,' he soothed. 'I'm not going to hurt you. I'm just going to rub your thigh and foot. You're so tense down here! Is there that much pain?'

'It is aching quite a bit, but it's nothing I can't handle. Oh . . .' she hissed, tensing again, trying to trust him, '. . . don't——'

'Leslie,' he murmured, and his hands rested warmly on her foot, now bare of sock and shoe. 'Calm down. I don't want to hurt you, I want to help you feel good. When I have ever been anything but gentle?'

She was much struck by that. 'Well, yes, I see what you mean,' she told him, lifting her head and peering over her shoulder at him. He was smiling, and his sparkling eyes met hers. They looked at each other for a long moment, each completely understanding the other's thought, and then Leslie put her head back down and closed her eyes.

His hands very carefully rubbed at the thigh muscles, manipulating her flesh into relaxation. Then he moved down to below the bandage, caressing her slim ankle and rubbing the bottom of her foot with the ball of his thumb. 'Is that helping at all?'

She groaned in pleasurable answer as she felt the constant grip of pain's tension ease away. 'It sure does. I hadn't realised how tense I was holding myself. Mmm, that's marvellous.' After working on her right leg, he then worked on her left, and she felt like boneless jelly, she was so wonderfully relaxed. Warm sexual awareness pierced her, and she rolled over abruptly, shying away from it, again. What was this need that she kept feeling? She questioned him, as she narrowed blue eyes that were nearly black, 'You were saying something, a few minutes ago, and then you stopped. You said "If only——" and I wonder how you would have finished the statement. How would it have ended?'

He smiled easily. 'Did I say that? I don't remember.' He was lying blatantly, and they both knew it. Leslie suddenly realised that he had made a mistake and was angry at himself for it.

She smiled slowly. 'Could you have possibly meant: "If only Jarred and I had got to you sooner?"'

He sat back, the light from the kitchen catching at the edges of his silver blond hair, throwing his face into dark brown shadow. It triggered a blurred memory in her mind; she straightened a little, alertly. 'Now what in the world would make you think a thing like that?' he returned blandly. She thought he smiled a little. 'Weren't you running a fever from your wound, and delirious?'

She replied softly. 'That's what I was told. But I could have sworn that you and Jarred were the ones who broke into the room when the leader of the group was questioning me. That couldn't have happened really, could it?' She watched him closely. Absolutely nothing flickered across his features.

'Now, what do you think?' he returned calmly. 'You know that after taking off, a radio message for help was sent to Florida.'

'Yes, that was also what I was told,' she said, sighing. 'And the authorities moved fast, barely an hour passing by before the island was invaded.'

'Which was lucky for you,' he told her, tapping her on the nose. She chuckled reluctantly. Scott then went back to massaging her legs, and by that time she was so used to the curiously sexless and yet intimately sensual body rub, that she was profoundly surprised when he reached forward and tenderly kissed the side of her slim ankle. The slender foot he was cupping quivered, and he continued to kiss her up to her skin, and to her knee, and the inside of her lower thigh. She started to tremble all over, for it wasn't particularly that he was kissing her bare leg, but how he was kissing

her, for he looked as if he meant each kiss very
deeply.

She reached forward to unbutton his shirt, but
he stopped her. 'No,' he said firmly, gently. That
shocked her more than anything else.

She leaned back and stared at him with
narrowed eyes. 'You want me,' she said softly,
though no betraying expression had crossed his
face. 'Why not?'

'I am not interested in having sex,' he said
patiently. 'I am quite mature. I know how to
handle my bodily urges now. You still don't
understand me, do you?' Incredibly, sadness crept
into his eyes as she stared at him. He reached over
and stroked her hair. 'Poor Leslie.'

She jerked her head back. 'No more body rubs,'
she uttered tersely.

He stood immediately. 'Fine.' She stared up at him.

'You just did it again, didn't you?' she accused.
'What was I to learn this time?'

He just laughed as he stood looking down at
her, shaking his head. And somehow the laughter
was the sadness too, the sadness that hadn't yet
left his eyes, and yet it was quite genuine
amusement. 'Good night, Les,' he said softly, and
walked into his bedroom, still laughing. She
couldn't believe her eyes and ears, as the door shut
behind him.

She swore explosively at the door, and then was
profoundly surprised when she started to laugh
herself.

*   *   *

The next few days were not quite as tangled as the first few had been. Scott still spoiled Leslie outrageously. Instead of getting used to the special treatment, she became more and more flustered as time went by. She could see genuine enjoyment as he did it, and knew that he was deriving a great deal of personal satisfaction out of her reaction. There was amusement, too, admittedly on both sides, rueful on her part, wicked on his. There was something else too, but she couldn't define it. She caught him watching her occasionally, with a look of something bittersweet and, oddly, pain. But the look always vanished before she could study it.

He taught her how to play poker, and she was a terrible player. They had an uproarious time as she made mistake after mistake, each one worse than the one before. She thought he would never recover his breath, when she asked him once what to do with four of a kind.

She looked around and found a pen and some paper, and then drew out a chequered board. They then played checkers, with pieces of torn paper, and chess, with the figures drawn with comical grotesqueness in miniature. She found Scott to be very astute, and soon there was a real competitiveness in their games, and they would let the board sit out all day, contemplating it from time to time, each victory hard won and never begrudged. If either one beat the other in the game of logic and strategy, they had deserved to win. Leslie was a challenging opponent.

'I like how your mind works,' he told her admiringly, after she beat him in a particularly long and involved game. The board had been out all afternoon, and each move had been agonised over, each chess piece lost with a groan of dismay.

'Thank you,' she returned, grinning lopsidedly. She was moving around with a greater ease now, and the leg didn't throb quite so much. 'Actually,' she told him, sipping at iced tea, 'my mind doesn't work.'

'Oh?' he laughingly asked, bending forward to tickle her bare foot.

'Cut that out. I play a lot on instinct. Isn't that silly? Sometimes I think things through laboriously, figuring out every consequence of every potential move, but sometimes I just do what feels right. It's my Achilles heel; now you'll beat me every time.'

'Oh, I doubt that. Your instincts are good, otherwise you wouldn't trust them like you do. I'd seen that about you, anyway, so you weren't telling me anything drastically new.'

'Is that so?' She bent forward and trickled cold liquid down his bare shin. He jumped and shifted sharply.

'Watch it, you little pervert!' she was reprimanded. She choked with laughter. He continued, 'Yes, I did. You screw your face up when you think it through, and when a possibility occurs to you, you cock your eyebrow as if to say, "Is that so?"' He mimicked her perfectly, and she threw her pillow at him.

'I don't.'

'You do, I swear it.'

She looked at him consideringly, eyes sharp. The bruises had faded, and vivacity had returned to her face, making her blue eyes seem even more blue, sparkling bright, her hair glistening healthily. 'I do use my head occasionally,' she commented casually, tilting back her head, eyes narrowed, lips hovering in an elusive smile.

'Well, now, I'm glad to hear it,' was his hearty response, and she had to laugh again.

But she sobered quickly enough, and she continued chattily. 'Yes, I can put two and two together, if it hits me in the face hard enough. I know why you brought me out here.'

He was very still, his regard sparkling dark, and she felt alive under that steady gaze. She smiled twistedly, and she could tell by the slight twitch of his lips that he was intrigued by her odd expression. 'And what conclusion have you come to?' he asked carefully, after a moment.

'You are trying to make something up to me,' Leslie replied, still watching him closely. 'You feel ashamed for leaving me on the island. You want to make it up to me. You think that I would not respect you for not having stayed, for not having made some attempt to make sure I was not dead, or making some attempt to save my life if I wasn't dead, because you knew that I would be killed shortly, like as not.'

He slouched in his chair, broad shoulders hunched, legs kicked out, eyes hooded. 'And is that how you see me?' he asked quietly.

'Oh, Scott!' she said, on a half moan, and then she laughed. His glance shot quickly to her, and she realised that he saw nothing funny in the situation. 'If you hadn't given yourself away already, you would have just now! Even if I don't understand a lot about you, and even if I don't know very much about your past life, I know enough to realise that if you really had boarded that plane, right now you would be feeling like dirt! You would be so ashamed of yourself, that you wouldn't be able to help mentioning it to me, apologising—you'd be acting totally different than you are right now—you wouldn't be able to look me so steadily in the face, like you are! You didn't go, and you won't ever be able to convince me that you did. I wasn't that delirious! You stayed, didn't you?'

'What do you think?' he asked softly, and she was exasperated by the usual question instead of answer, even as she was taken by surprise at the steady, warm glow of something in his eyes that held her expression.

He was seated in the armchair, which was pulled around so that he could prop his legs on the coffee table. She was lounging on the couch opposite him, and she got up to come around the coffee table, easing down into a kneeling position beside the chair, watching him as he watched her so attentively, head turned to her, patient. She leaned her arms on the arm rest and bent forward, to stare at him eye to eye.

'What I think,' she whispered, 'is that you were

feeling so utterly furious, and so furiously helpless, that by the time you saw me struggling with the guard just outside the barrack, you'd just about had it. You leapt through the window and didn't care if anyone did hear the glass break. You threw everything out the window when you jumped, because you just couldn't stand to see me get raped. You risked everything, when you jumped, and it wasn't just thirty hostages' lives that I'm talking about, was it?'

'Because I've been thinking, and I've thought of the "commander" and the People's Revolutionary Republic and that they really didn't make too much sense when they hijacked the plane, any more than you have on that subject, or anyone else. I'm thinking that they must have had something on board so valuable that they would risk many lives to get it out of the United States. Perhaps it was something to do with smuggling. If they had been smuggling marijuana into the States and found they couldn't get out again because of increased policing in Florida—that would make sense, or really anything: industrial information, state secrets, any kind of illegal drugs. I'm also thinking that there were a few "journalists" who were more than they seemed at the time. You were the one who found me, who shot and killed the commander after the plane had taken off, weren't you?'

Only a few inches away, his eyes were looking into hers hard, face calm and relaxed, and yet something quivered through him at her question, something that made her stare, the embers of a murderous rage remembered. He said uncompromisingly, 'Yes.'

She pressed on. 'You would have rather died than leave me, or anyone else, on that island while you left freely, wouldn't you?'

His eyes glittered. She caught her breath at the leaping emotion in those expressive eyes. 'Yes.'

'Your earlier silence betrays you,' she murmured, watching him with very bright, keenly intelligent eyes. 'Was there something illegal on that plane, something that you haven't the freedom to discuss, something for which the People's Revolutionary Republic was only a front?'

Deadly serious. 'Yes.'

'This is incredible. You and Jarred—Scott,' she asked unsteadily, 'who do you work for?'

Sudden, vivid amusement. His shoulders quivered with mirth. 'Only the newspaper, Les. I didn't tell you that I've taken a promotion offer while you were in the hospital, did I? You're looking at the newest editor on the *Times* staff.'

She felt stunned. She sniffed the air like a hunting hound. 'I can't be that wrong,' she muttered, staring at him thoughtfully. 'You and Jarred stayed, only you two. Wayne would have tried to stay. I mentioned something to him, and he had been furious for some reason. He wouldn't have left me either, any more than you would have, but he did because he was forced to. You forced him, didn't you?'

He was still laughing silently, watching her, no reply.

'Your silence betrays you again,' she mused, propping her chin on one hand and regarding him. 'If I was off target, if I was that wrong about you two, your natural reaction would be to expostulate, to tell me "Of course not, don't be ridiculous!" But you aren't saying it, and yet you don't talk. It must have been the way I asked the question.' She thought and then phrased her next question carefully. 'Were you ever at one time employed by the government in a capacity that you are not at liberty to discuss?'

Scott didn't lie. He smiled and said nothing.

CHAPTER NINE

INSTEAD he asked her a question, as he reached out a forefinger and traced her cheek lightly. A shiver tickled down her spine. 'Are you changed by what happened on the island?'

She jerked. 'You understand me that well?' was her reply. She sighed and rubbed at her eyes. 'Yes, I think so. I . . . it all happened so fast! I was scared, threatened, repulsed, exhilarated, dismayed . . . I was so many things with so many people in such a short space of time! It was most unsettling.'

'You were beaten, shot, hijacked,' he continued for her gently. 'You had to fight for your life and for other people's lives. You had to act under terrible pressure, and you were horribly alone——'

'And in some ways I'd never felt so violently aware in all my life,' she finished, with a strange laugh. He watched her carefully. 'Do you know, there for a while I was racing along, my mind working at a fantastic speed, the adrenalin flowing, my pulse pounding. I could have died several times, but I was so alive!'

'Some people collapse under those kind of circumstances. You rose to meet the occasion and survived. It's a theme replayed throughout mankind's history. Man—meets the elements and

168

survives them, and sometimes surpasses all expectations.' This was a new side to the man that Leslie was coming to know, a contemplative, deep side. He looked oddly ageless, sitting there so quietly in the armchair, hands still, eyes attentive, mind active. As she watched him, she was struck by the physical beauty in the harmonious blend of dark golden brown tan and lighter shade of hair, with the chocolate of his eyes and the silver flashing highlights at the edges of his head. She had a fleeting, strange impression of a young man with the same irregular features, minus the mature lines, with a more reckless gleam in his eyes. Then she also saw an older man, a quieter man, with the silver blond hair becoming more silver than blond, with his strong, gentle hands gnarling, and his eyes even more compassionate. She saw and realised that they were all the same man, what he was and what he was capable of becoming. She wondered that Dennis had only seen her for what she'd been in the past, too blind to see what she was becoming, herself. Then grief hit her briefly, as she knew again that she would never see Jenny as a beautiful, mature young woman.

'Why,' she asked suddenly, 'did you accept the promotion, Scott? What made you quit your other job, your journalistic work with Jarred? You are such a talented writer, and you had such a gift for finding information!'

He looked beyond her, to the shadows in the corner of the living room. The summer heat still brooded in the night. She wiped a trickle of sweat

from her hairline and shifted in her suddenly
cramped position. He noticed, stood, and helped
her to the couch. She was grateful for his
thoughtfulness, as her leg had stiffened up. Just as
she was getting miserable, wondering if he meant
to rebuff this question also, he sighed. She tensed.
It was so terribly important.

'I'm older, Les. I'm thirty-eight, I have been
galloping all over the world for eight years, and
before that I'd fought like a mad dog in the
business game, thrashing to get to the top,' he said
quietly. He was still looking away from her, into
something that only he could see. She felt a sharp
pang and then sudden fierce tenderness. He wasn't
getting old. He was young still! He was strong,
upright—she felt a constriction in her throat as she
realised that she wasn't the only one to see the
future. 'I'm no longer so very young that I feel an
endless abundance of vitality and arrogance. I
see—sometimes—the consequences of my actions.'
He eased himself down on the couch beside her
and absently took her hand, caressing it and
looking down wryly at the fingers he fondled. 'I
killed a man last week,' he said, as if he were
talking about the weather. The feeling in her
throat went to her chest and the tightness got even
tighter. 'I won't pretend that he is necessarily the
first man I've ever shot. You would only disbelieve
me if I did, and there's no point in it. But this time
it was different. I knew that morning that
everything was going to be all right, when we
found one of the men who said that the

commander was still questioning you. You were alive, and he was going to die. Oh, yes, I was very sure of that. I exploded into the room, and drew up the machine gun.' The constriction in her chest was a leaden thing, and she covered her mouth to hide her trembling lips. Memory was bright and blurry, and it all was real, the sickness, the rage, the fear, the big blond man who crashed into her life just when she had thought it over.

Scott turned his head and took in her discomposure. As she looked up at him he smiled such a sweet and tender smile of compassion for her unpleasant memories that she couldn't contain the wet drop that trembled a moment on spiked brown lashes before slipping away. 'You see,' he told her softly, 'I pulled the trigger with such a savage, destructive joy, I could barely see. It was all so wonderfully glorious, his bleeding body slumping against the opposite wall, and my surging feeling of triumph. I'd saved you; he was dead; I had won. I have to live with that. Not really that he was killed, mind you: the man was in a corner. He would have fought before surrendering, and he would have lost. And it wasn't even that I was the man who killed him. No, Leslie, what I have to live with is that one, overwhelming moment of unholy joy as I took the man's life away from him forever. I did it with no regrets—if faced with the same situation, I would do the same, with as much primitive, amoral glee. I still feel that distant haze of red rage when I think of how I found you, bloody, beaten, hopeless and

helpless—so vulnerable that I could have crushed
you with one hand, and so like a battered child.
It's done, finished, to my great and intense
satisfaction. But never in my life will I hold a gun
again.'

She felt so stricken; she felt so utterly shaken,
she didn't know if she would ever feel steady
again; she looked at him, eyes huge, mute. She
didn't understand why, but she suddenly knew
that in some way she didn't yet quite comprehend,
this man had brought her entire life to a standstill
and nothing would ever be the same again.

He looked at her, and he didn't say anything.
He let her see, without prevarication, what was
deep in those dark, shadowed orbs. He was steady,
unashamed of what he was, and it was Leslie who
looked away first. She didn't see the look of both
pain and deep emotion that invaded those steady
eyes, for she was looking down at her hand,
clasped so tenderly in his own stronger ones. She
watched him raise her hand to his lips, quivered as
he pressed a soft kiss to her palm, watched as he
stood and whispered, 'Sleep well, Leslie.'

He let go of her hand and it fell to her lap, quite
unnoticed. She watched him turn and walk silently
to his room, shutting the door behind him, such a
quiet man, so deep and philosophical, an'
accepting of himself, what he was.

He was a better person than she, for that. The
sanctimonious, self-righteous guilt she had
whipped herself with for the one night of
indiscretion, that mistake that had been a mistake

simply because of her outlook and attitude—she
had besmirched a night that should have been a
good, rare memory, for the tawdry morality had
been in existence in her mind only, never his. She
now understood his anger and underlying hurt at
her behaviour stemming from that night, and his
bafflement. He wouldn't understand what she'd
been doing, couldn't understand because she
hadn't explained. Her hypocritical morality that
told her she could enjoy sex with a husband she
might not have loved, but not a man with whom
she had shared a night of love but not a lifetime
commitment—it all flashed through her mind as
she listened to the silence from without and heeded
the voices within.

The beast had stirred and whispered, and she
had heeded its prodding. The beast was not
necessarily bad and not particularly good, though
sometimes, violently, both. To be human meant to
merely bear the burden of the self, with dignity, if
possible.

For a long, long time she sat there and felt the
weight and the wonder that was herself.

She stood, and her leg had stiffened again,
which made walking awkward and painful.
Somehow, though, the pain was something she
could revel in, a physical part of the life she was
experiencing. She shut the front door, turned off
the living room light, and leaned against the wall
for a long moment while her eyes adjusted to the
darkness. Everything was in shadow, dark upon
dark, but she need not have any fears for what lay

ahead of her. It was all in the same place as in the light, only seen and felt differently.

Her eyes soon could pick out the various shapes of things. When she could discern, she walked haltingly to the closed door that was his. Her hand went out, grasped the doorknob, turned it silently. The door opened; there was no lock. She slipped quietly to the side of his bed and looked down on his sleeping form. His chest was bare, sheets tangled roughly around his hips, one dark leg thrown out from under, his head turned away to the wall. She thought she could see the rise and fall of his chest as he breathed, but she wasn't sure in the enveloping darkness. It didn't matter, for she knew with every breath she took that he also breathed, and that was a good feeling. He was so large as he lay there sleeping, and so strong and still, and so vulnerable underneath the strength and determination. He was a man, a splendid man, who lived a sincerity in his code of life that was wonderful to see.

Leslie sat very gently down on the side of his bed, and as the mattress shifted to take her weight, his head moved and she knew that he was awake. He stayed still and waited, silently. She reached out a tentative hand and placed it on his chest, feeling the warmth and the silk of his skin that covered hard bone and sinewy muscle and keen personality. She touched him, and the touch became a stroke as he stiffened and became rigid, unmoving. She thought she saw a faint glitter from his eyes. Then she reached down and touched her lips to him, and her lips were warm on his warmth, soft skin on skin. She caressed him, and he drew a sharp, shaking, audible breath. Her hand heaved in movement with his chest, and she lifted it to lean over him and put her fingers lightly against the side of his cheek, trailing them down to his jaw, slight prickling roughness against sensitive fingertips, and then to his mouth, the edge of her fingernail catching on his lower lip. He opened his mouth to say something, but she hastened to put her hand over his mouth to still whatever it was.

She whispered, a soft sound in a silent place, 'I don't want to have sex. I am a mature woman and know how to control my bodily urges. I want to make love, beautiful, warm, passionate, sharing love. I want to make love to you.' She hesitated, fingers sliding away. Silence, a sheet rustle, a sigh. She wasn't sure who had sighed. Then she trembled, as he made no move but stared at her, head half lifted off the pillow, dark gold hair falling on to stark white. 'Please—do you want me to go?'

Paralysed moment, and then sudden, surging movement. He came up, his arms coming out and overwhelmingly surrounding her, drawing her to that silken hard warmth, bare against her cheek. He drew her down and rose above her, and removed her clothes. She held his head to her.

CHAPTER TEN

A week passed. The sun disappeared behind a horrendous wall of lowering clouds for a time and then came out to smile again. Leslie limped less, felt better, her bruises faded, and her energy returned. The summer air brooded, heavy and ominous, and the silence became oppressive. Scott was quiet, always there, always in her consciousness. They didn't talk much. They made love sometimes, leisurely. Leslie slept a lot. Once Scott went out in the car for food supplies. She didn't bother accompanying him. He wouldn't have accepted help from her anyway.

Instead of basking in the permeating serenity of the silence shrouded forest, Leslie was tensing up, becoming restless, feeling constricted. Scott's silent attitude was wearing on her nerves. She found herself watching him: noting the film of sweat on his silken brown chest when he went without a shirt in the summer heat; studying his firm lips as he tilted his head back for a long cool drink from a tall iced tea glass; watching his neck muscles work. She was intensely aware of his body, and this increased as time went by, instead of dissipating.

Scott wasn't quite as good natured as he seemed, either, she found, when he snapped at her for no apparent reason. She stared up at him, feeling astonishingly hurt, as tears welled up in her dark blue eyes. He sighed, rubbing the back of his neck as if it pained him, and then apologised lowly.

Now she sat out on the porch and absently swatted at a mindless winged creature that repeatedly batted against her arm, and she pondered. The evening was well advanced, and she was in deep dusky shadow, for though the living room door was open, the light was off. Scott was in the lit kitchen, drinking coffee and reading. The faint glow thrown through the picture window was all the illumination she had. Funny, she thought. She couldn't remember the last time she just sat, by herself, and listened to the sounds of night.

Thoughts welled up, and shouted at each other. You're crazy to be here, something whispered. Something else murmured, he's just inside. Another voice asked, where are you going next? She shied away from the thoughts and lifted her cotton top away from her chest. She was so warm. Something rumbled darkly, off in the darkness. Trees swayed in the rising wind, and the breeze felt oddly cool against her damp skin. It would storm.

Why do I feel so tormented? she asked the dark.

Scott looked up as she walked into the kitchen's circle of light, and he smiled. He was leaning back in his chair, legs propped on the one other chair, with faded denim shorts on and nothing else. She knew now how he managed to stay so brown, for he spent time outside nearly every day, either

jogging or cleaning away fallen branches from the
cabin's clearing or doing some kind of physical
exercise. His smile faded and a faintly questioning
look came into his eyes as she walked slowly up to
him, took away his book and put it on the table.
He cocked his head whimsically and looked up at
her.

Her eyes utterly serious and oddly desperate, she
regarded him silently. Then she reached down and
placed her hands on his shoulders, bending
forward to kiss him on the mouth. He tilted his
head back and willingly responded. She pushed
past the barrier of his lips and deepened the kiss
erotically, while her hands strayed, feather light,
down his bare chest to caress the flat muscles of
his stomach.

His hands went to hers, but whether he meant to
push her away or press her hands to him, she
never knew, for she suddenly dragged away from
him and sat down in a slump across the table from
him, in the chair his legs had been on. They stared
at each other. His gaze was arrested, but not
surprised, she noted.

'It's no use,' she sighed, weary, rubbing at her
eyes. He was receptively still, only his eyes moving,
on her, attentive, masked.

'What's no use?' he asked her.

'This, you, me—everything.' She shrugged, a
helpless movement. Then, before she could help
herself, the question welled up again, born of
frustration. 'What do you want from me?'

'Will you stop asking me that question?' he

suddenly exploded, wrathfully. 'Why are you always so worried about what I might ask of you?'

The sigh she emitted was gusty, bitten off. She just stared at him, eyes widened. 'My whole life, everyone has wanted something from me. Be this, don't do that—be my wife, be a good daughter, don't, for God's sake, do anything foolish! Well, I can handle that. I know what they want from me, and I know what I can give them. But you! This! Oh, I knew what to expect from you at the very first, and I could handle that too, but so much has happened and everything's changed. I don't know the rules to this game, and I don't know what you want!'

'I have never made demands on you,' he said, from between clenched teeth. His hands were in fists.

'Yes, and for some reason that's worse than anything!' she burst out, oddly near to tears. 'You kidnap me, bring me here, and you watch and wait. Always waiting, and for what? You refuse to tell me about your past. You take care of me and refuse to let me lift a finger. You—you're—this is driving me crazy!'

He stood slowly and she watched him rise up. His face was rock-granite hard, the bones compressed, as if he were exercising an immense control over extreme emotion. 'All right,' he said flatly. 'You want answeres, you'll get answers. You just couldn't leave it, could you? You just couldn't accept what I was trying to offer you for a time. I have never been married, nor in the past have I wanted to be married. I have been what I wished, and where I wished, and I've travelled whenever I liked. I have done a great many things, some of which I am proud of, others that I am not so proud of. One night I met you. It was a sultry evening, hot and humid, and you were like a bright, flickering flame, vivid and flashing. I wanted you and I had you.'

A week earlier she might have flinched at the bald words. Now she only stared back at him shaken, but meeting his eyes. There was something molten there, at the back of his hard front. She began to wonder what she had stirred up by her questions and suddenly wasn't sure if she wanted to know.

Scott leaned forward on the table and his lips cocked mockingly as he interpreted the expressions flitting across her face. He looked down unblinkingly, his eyes compelling, forcing her to face him. 'You're a coward, Les,' he said softly. She felt slapped. 'Underneath that mask of wordly experience, you just can't face it. Tell me. Let me hear the words, that's all it takes. Tell me to shut up and I'll shut up.'

She stood so fast her chair crashed to the floor, and neither even noticed. She was now trembling so much she could barely support herself on her legs. 'I am no coward!' she screamed out, in a rage, and hurt. 'I am not a coward! How can you *say* that to me?'

'It's about time somebody said it to you!' he shouted back. 'Because that's what you are and have been ever since your husband died!'

The resounding echo of her slap bounded around the kitchen, confined between the walls, and she stared at the reddening mark on his cheek, utterly appalled at herself. His expression never changed. He hadn't even flinched. 'Do it again, if it makes you feel good,' he told her pleasantly. His eyes glittered, and the molten rage was to the fore. 'But next time, Les, I slap back.'

Now she was frightened, and she whispered, 'Oh, I'm sorry.' But again his expression never changed, and she turned to hurry out of the kitchen, hands over her mouth. She was jerked around to face a very angry man. 'Let me go!' she cried out, trying to twist out of his hands.

He threw her into the armchair and she cried out again as she slammed into the cushions. He pinned her in the seat by putting his two hands on either arm rest, and he leaned over her, too close and overwhelmingly large. She shrank away, eyes twin huge pools in a white face.

'I've changed my mind now. You're going to have to listen to me one way or another, you aren't going to stop me now,' he whispered, and she fully believed him. He was looking as inevitable as death. 'You left after that night without a word, and I was furious when I woke up. I came after you, determined to get an explanation, some kind of reason for your behaviour, and I met a totally different woman from the one I'd known before. I was baffled. I wanted to get to know you better, to understand. You refused. Then we left on assignment and everything fell apart. And suddenly I was meeting another Leslie, a courageous woman, and I didn't know who was the real you. Were you the whore you pretended to me, or were you the hard bitten career woman? And where did the Leslie on the island fit in? Everything about you threw me off, and I couldn't see the truth, no matter how I tried.

'Then you took that desperate chance, and I was convinced you were the whore after all, and I was sick. But Wayne reacted totally differently and it was only then that I found out you'd been married, had once, in fact, had a family. It was only then that I started to understand a little more about you, as the jigsaw pieces started to fall into place.

'You were right about me being unable to leave you. You were more accurate than you could know. Something had snapped that night when I saw you on the ground, fighting for not only your own life, but also ours.' He suddenly shifted his hands and gripped her head, palms on either side, fingers gripping into her hair. Caught, she held herself perfectly still, unable to get away, turn her head, stop her ears. 'I found I loved you, that night. I told you the other day, when I told of my joy in murdering the beast that was hurting you so badly, only you were either too dense to hear, or you didn't want to know.' The words were whispered bitterly; they sounded to her to be shouted directly into her shrinking heart, reverberating in a shock wave.

He let go of her suddenly and walked away, and

that too shocked her so that she couldn't move. He went to the screen door and looked out into the night, his back to her. 'I brought you here,' he said unemotionally, 'because I cared. I hated to see you bruised, and I wanted to give you time here to enjoy the quiet and the serenity of the place. I kidnapped you because I thought it important enough to ride over your inevitable prevarications and protestations. I waited on you because I wanted you to heal from your wound. I kept quiet because I didn't want to make you feel like you had to talk about your past, which was so obviously painful to you.'

Dear heaven, she thought faintly. When the shocks come, they keep coming and coming. Her whole life had been thrown into chaos and, like the inside of a clothes drier, everything kept tumbling over and over, and she didn't know if she would ever find her way out of it again. Huddled in the chair, horribly exposed, she held her arms around her chest in a defensive gesture, wholly unconscious of it. She watched as Scott turned and looked at her, his face all at once very tired.

'Look at you,' he said, on a half laugh. 'You're backed in a corner, with your arms around yourself for protection. You didn't want anyone to make a fool of himself over you. You want to be footloose, completely carefree in a way you were never allowed to be. God, Leslie—you're such a strange woman—you make me feel at once infuriated with your obtuseness and protective because you're so damned vulnerable! You don't

have to tell me. I know you don't want it, you
didn't ask for it! You've got to go out and find the
next adventure, run away to look at a new
horizon. You have to play like a child. Well, I'm
through with playing. I had to stop. We're at two
different points in our lives, but I have never, ever
wanted to tie you down or stifle any part of you.
I'd never planned on saying any of this. It all just
had to come out.'

He walked slowly over to her and bent to
crouch before her. She sat like stone, afraid to
move for fear the action might shift everything in
her world yet again. He picked up her hands and
kissed her fingers so tenderly that she could barely
stand it, for he'd been giving her the truth, and
giving her so much of himself, and he kept on
giving and just couldn't see how that shook her up
so.

'I have to tell you,' he murmured softly, eyes
huge and dark with the burden of his unflinching
honesty, 'that I did have one wild, unquenchable
hope. You mustn't feel that I'm saying it to push
you to anything you don't wish. I've cherished
what you were able to give to me while you stayed
here these last several days.' He spoke as if she
were leaving, she thought. How did he know she
was going to leave him? But she knew the answer
to that. He'd always seen more of her than she'd
been able to see of him. 'But, Leslie, I had hoped
against hope that maybe—just maybe—you might
grow to know me and love me back in some way.'
He stood abruptly. 'The keys are still on the

counter. I'll give you directions to get back. You wouldn't remember the way since you slept most of the drive up. Drive carefully, and if you want to come back later on, you'll be welcome. You'll always be welcome. If you would, ask Wayne to come up at the end of the month. He said he'd pick me up if I needed it. Goodnight, darling. I'll see you off in the morning.'

And that was it. She was left looking after him, searching frantically for something well adjusted and meaningful to say. Nothing came, and he closed his door on her, leaving her all alone.

She eventually dragged herself off to her own room, instinctively knowing that his was quite off limits now. She didn't even notice Jenny and Dennis as they looked out into the room, laughing frozenly.

It stormed in the night, wind and rain lashing at the window, bright lightning flashing spasmodically, burning into her retina as she tossed and turned sleeplessly. What was wrong with her? He had asked nothing, absolutely nothing of her. She was totally free of commitment. She was leaving in the morning. She told herself that over and over.

The morning was fresh washed and dewy clean. The sun sparkled over the greens and browns and a piercing sky blue as she looked outside, and for some reaon the beauty of it hurt her eyes. She turned away and went back to her packing. Movement was automatic. She certainly knew how

to pack. She carried her suitcases out to the car
and put them in the back seat. She was going back
to her life, the one she had worked so hard to
build and was working so desperately now to
preserve. She couldn't wait to know where she
would be going next. All of those exotic countries,
different, explosive, challenging, stimulating. The
words were a dull litany in her mind as she stared
around at the by now hauntingly familiar clearing.
That oak over there, good for leaning against in
the shade. The wooden porch that she'd dreamed
on in the summer night's heat. That window that
was Scott's. She had been up very early because of
her sleepless night, and hadn't seen him. She
wondered if he was expecting her to say goodbye.

She couldn't seem to get into the car. Oh, the
adventures she would have! She told herself she
couldn't wait. She slowly managed to get behind
the wheel, her limbs oddly working as though
under water. She leaned her head on the steering
wheel and put her hands behind her head.

Why was she feeling so lost? Surely this was not
love, this ache and this confusion. Surely she had
been smart enough to avoid that trap, having
fallen in once. Once bitten, twice shy. Surely she
was in just a phase! As soon as she was on the
road, with the wind in her hair and the open
country before her, everything would, indeed, be
different. But when she thought of it, the worse
she felt until she thought she would be swallowed
up in the misery.

She lifted her head and stared at her reflection in

the windshield. Ah, what an idiot she was! She was going to get out of the car, she knew it. She was going to walk back into that house and make an utter fool of herself for the second time in her life. She was going to tie herself to a man, and she was going to strengthen those ties every chance she got. She was going to love him like he'd never been loved before, and she was going to laugh with him and share her sorrows and her joys. She was going to lean on him when she was weak, and let him lean on her when he needed her to be strong. She was going to have to share her drawer space and the toothpaste, and sometimes forego watching her favourite television programme so that he could see the baseball game. She would come home and have someone waiting for her, welcoming her. She would be this miserable every time she left, yearning to be with the man, thinking of him as she did her job, feeling that half joy, half sorrow as she was by herself and fulfilling her intellectual needs. She was going to share her sometimes painful growth with him, and watch him mature also. They were going to quarrel, and cry, and then make up with a mutual relief and joy that would overwhelm them both. They were going to make love in all its various moods: violently, tenderly, leisurely, urgently. She was going to wash his socks, and he would cook the special meals.

Her sudden rich laughter welled up from the surprisingly deep welling of joy that flooded her. Yes, indeed, what marvellous fools they would be, together. Always together.

She got out of the car and bounded up the porch steps, ignoring the twinges in her leg in her eagerness. She crossed the porch in two long strides and threw open the front door. She lightly crossed to his door, and it was open. He was sitting on his made bed, his head in his hands, the fingers pushed into the silken silver blond hair, his powerful shoulders hunched, an attitude of utter dejection. He was dressed. At the sound of her footfall on the threshold, his head reared up and as he looked at her, his eyes widened.

She was lithe and laughing, her blue eyes brilliant, her face vivid and wonderfully alive with the glow of joy within. Her mouth was pulled into a wide and sunny smile, the smile she'd given once to a daughter, if she had but known it. The message was written plainly across her face and in her eager approach, and he looked as if he couldn't believe it. 'Hello,' she greeted him, and he had to stand abruptly as she threw herself into his arms and wound her own around his neck firmly. 'Did you miss me? I'm home.'

She'd told him everything in that simple greeting, and in her expressive, loving smile. She watched as exultation leapt into living flames in his glowing dark eyes. He bent his head.

Harlequin Presents

Coming Next Month

Available in March wherever paperback books are sold, or through
Harlequin Reader Service:

In the U.S.
901 Fuhrmann Blvd.
P.O. Box 1397
Buffalo, N.Y. 14240-1397

In Canada
P.O. Box 603
Fort Erie, Ontario
L2A 5X3

MAIL-IN-OFFER
OFFER CERTIFICATE ✄

I have enclosed the required number of proofs of purchase from any specially marked "Gifts From The Heart" Harlequin romance book, plus cash register receipts and a check or money order payable to Harlequin Gifts From The Heart Offer, to cover postage and handling.

002

CHECK ONE	ITEM	# OF PROOFS OF PURCHASE	POSTAGE & HANDLING FEE
	01 Brass Picture Frame	2	$ 1.00
	02 Heart-Shaped Candle Holders with Candles	3	$ 1.00
	03 Heart-Shaped Keepsake Box	4	$ 1.00
	04 Gold-Plated Heart Pendant	5	$ 1.00
	05 Collectors' Doll Limited quantities available	12	$ 2.75

NAME _____

STREET ADDRESS _____ APT. # _____

CITY _____ STATE _____ ZIP _____

Mail this certificate, designated number of proofs of purchase (inside back page) and check or money order for postage and handling to:

Gifts From The Heart, P.O. Box 4814
Reidsville, N. Carolina 27322-4814

NOTE THIS IMPORTANT OFFER'S TERMS

Requests must be postmarked by May 31, 1988. Only proofs of purchase from specially marked "Gifts From The Heart" Harlequin books will be accepted. This certificate plus cash register receipts and a check or money order to cover postage and handling must accompany your request and may not be reproduced in any manner. Offer void where prohibited, taxed or restricted by law. LIMIT ONE REQUEST PER NAME, FAMILY, GROUP, ORGANIZATION OR ADDRESS. Please allow up to 8 weeks after receipt of order for shipment. Offer only good in the U.S.A. Hurry—Limited quantities of collectors' doll available. Collectors' dolls will be mailed to first 15,000 qualifying submitters. All other submitters will receive 12 free previously unpublished Harlequin books and a postage & handling refund.

OFFER-1RR

ATTRACTIVE, SPACE SAVING BOOK RACK

Display your most prized novels on this handsome and sturdy book rack. The hand-rubbed walnut finish will blend into your library decor with quiet elegance, providing a practical organizer for your favorite hard-or soft-covered books.

Only $9.95

Approximately 16" x 8" when assembled

Assembles in seconds!

To order, rush your name, address and zip code, along with a check or money order for $10.70* ($9.95 plus 75¢ postage and handling) payable to *Harlequin Reader Service*:

Harlequin Reader Service
Book Rack Offer
901 Fuhrmann Blvd.
P.O. Box 1396
Buffalo, NY 14269-1396

Offer not available in Canada.

BKR-1A

*New York and Iowa residents add appropriate sales tax.

GIFTS FROM THE HEART
from *Harlequin*

FREE BY MAIL With proofs of purchase plus postage and handling

A. Hand-polished solid brass picture frame 1-5/8″ × 1-3/8″ with 2 proofs of purchase.

B. Individually handworked, pair of heart-shaped glass candle holders (2″ diameter), 6″ candles included, with 3 proofs of purchase.

C. Heart-shaped porcelain keepsake box (1″ high) with delicate flower motif with 4 proofs of purchase.

D. Radiant gold-plated heart pendant on 16″ chain with complimentary satin pouch with 5 proofs of purchase.

E. Beautiful collectors' doll with genuine porcelain face, hands and feet, and a charming heart appliqué on dress with 12 proofs of purchase. Limited quantities available. See offer terms.

HERE IS HOW TO GET YOUR FREE GIFTS

Send us the required number of proofs of purchase (below) of specially marked ''Gifts From The Heart'' Harlequin books and cash register receipts with the Offer Certificate (available in the back pages) properly completed, plus a check or money order (do not send cash) payable to Harlequin Gifts From The Heart Offer. We'll RUSH you your specified gift. Hurry—Limited quantities of collectors' doll available. See offer terms.

101R

GIFTS FROM THE HEART
ONE PROOF OF PURCHASE

To collect your free gift by mail you must include the necessary number of proofs of purchase with order certificate.